THE FORGOTTEN WALTZ

BY THE SAME AUTHOR

FICTION

The Portable Virgin

The Wig My Father Wore

What Are You Like?

The Pleasure of Eliza Lynch

The Gathering

Yesterday's Weather

NON-FICTION

Making Babies

ANTHOLOGY

The Granta Book of the Irish Short Story (editor)

The Forgotten Waltz

Anne Enright

W. W. NORTON & COMPANY
NEW YORK | LONDON

First American Edition 2011

Printed in the United States of America

For information about permission to reproduce selections from this book,
write to Permissions, W. W. Norton & Company, Inc.,
500 Fifth Avenue, New York, NY 10110

For information about special discounts for bulk purchases, please contact
W. W. Norton Special Sales at specialsales@wwnorton.com or 800-233-4830

Manufacturing by Courier Westford
Book design by Beth Tondreau
Production manager: Louise Mattarelliano

Library of Congress Cataloging-in-Publication Data

Enright, Anne, 1962–
The forgotten waltz / Anne Enright. — 1st American ed.
p. cm.
ISBN 978-0-393-07255-6 (hardcover)
1. Marriage—Fiction. 2. Adultery—Fiction. 3. Families—Ireland—Fiction.
4. Dublin (Ireland)—Fiction. I. Title.
PR6055.N73F67 2011
823'.914—dc23
2011021006

W. W. Norton & Company, Inc.
500 Fifth Avenue, New York, N.Y. 10110
www.wwnorton.com

W. W. Norton & Company Ltd.
Castle House, 75/76 Wells Street, London W1T 3QT

1 2 3 4 5 6 7 8 9 0

PREFACE

IF IT HADN'T BEEN FOR THE CHILD then none of this might have happened, but the fact that a child was involved made everything that much harder to forgive. Not that there is anything to forgive, of course, but the fact that a child was mixed up in it all made us feel that there was no going back; that it mattered. The fact that a child was affected meant we had to face ourselves properly, we had to follow through.

She was nine when it started, but that hardly matters. I mean her age hardly matters because she was always special – isn't that the word? Of course all children are special, all children are beautiful. I always thought Evie was a bit peculiar, I have to say: but also that she was special in the old-fashioned sense of the word. There was a funny, off-centre beauty to her. She went to an ordinary school, but there was, even at that stage, an amount of ambivalence about Evie, the sense of things unsaid. Even the doctors – especially the doctors – kept it vague, with their, 'Wait and see.'

So there was a lot of anxiety around Evie – too much, I thought, because she was also a lovely child. When I got to know her better, I saw that she could be cranky, or lonely; I questioned her happiness. But when she was nine I thought of her as a beautiful, clear little person, a kind of gift, too.

And when she saw me kissing her father – when she saw her father kissing me, in his own house – she laughed and flapped her hands. A shrill, unforgettable hoot. It was a laugh, I thought later, mostly of recognition, but also of spite, or something like it – glee, perhaps. And her mother, who was just downstairs, said, 'Evie! What are you doing up there?' making the child glance back over her shoulder. 'Come on, down now.'

And some miracle of her mother's voice, so casual and controlled, made Evie think that everything was all right, despite the fact that I had been kissing her father. Not for the first time, either – though I now think of it as the first real time, the first official occasion of our love, on New Year's Day 2007, when Evie was still pretty much a child.

I

THERE WILL BE PEACE IN THE VALLEY

I MET HIM IN MY SISTER'S GARDEN in Enniskerry. That is where I saw him first. There was nothing fated about it, though I add in the late summer light and the view. I put him at the bottom of my sister's garden, in the afternoon, at the moment the day begins to turn. Half five maybe. It is half past five on a Wicklow summer Sunday when I see Seán for the first time. There he is, where the end of my sister's garden becomes uncertain. He is about to turn around – but he doesn't know this yet. He is looking at the view and I am looking at him. The sun is low and lovely. He is standing where the hillside begins its slow run down to the coast, and the light is at his back, and it is just that time of day when all the colours come into their own.

It is some years ago now. The house is new and this is my sister's housewarming party, or first party, a few months after they moved in. The first thing they did was take down the wooden fence, to get their glimpse of the sea, so the back of the house sits like a missing tooth in the row of new homes, exposed to the easterly winds and to curious cows; a little stage set, for this afternoon, of happiness.

They have new neighbours in, and old pals, and me, with a few cases of wine and the barbecue they put on their wedding list but ended up buying themselves. It sits on the patio, a green thing with a swivelling bucket of a lid, and my brother-in-law Shay – I think he even wore the apron – waves wooden tongs over lamb steaks and chicken drumsticks, while cracking cans of beer, high in the air, with his free hand.

Fiona keeps expecting me to help because I am her sister. She passes with an armful of plates and shoots me a dark look. Then she remembers that I am a guest and offers me some Chardonnay.

'Yes,' I say. 'Yes, I'd love some, thanks,' and we chat like grown-ups. The glass she fills me is the size of a swimming pool.

It makes me want to cry to think of it. It must have been 2002. There I was, just back from three weeks in Australia and mad – just *mad* – into Chardonnay. My niece Megan must have been four, my nephew nearly two: fantastic, messy little items, who look at me like they are waiting for the joke. They have friends in, too. It's hard to tell how many kids there are, running around the place – I think they are being cloned in the downstairs bathroom. A woman goes in there with one toddler and she always comes out fussing over two.

I sit beside the glass wall between the kitchen and garden – it really is a lovely house – and I watch my sister's life. The mothers hover round the table where the kids' food is set, while, out in the open air, the men sip their drinks and glance skywards, as though for rain. I end up talking to a woman who is sitting beside a plate of chocolate Rice Krispie cakes and working her way through them in a forgetful sort of way. They have mini-marshmallows on top. She goes to pop one in her mouth, then she pulls back in surprise.

'Ooh, pink!' she says.

I don't know what I was waiting for. My boyfriend, Conor, must have been dropping someone off or picking them up – I can't remember why he wasn't back. He would have been driving. He usually drove, so I could have a few drinks. Which was one of the good things about Conor, I have to say. These days, it's me who drives. Though that is an improvement, too.

And I don't know why I remember the chocolate Rice Krispies, except that 'Ooh, pink!' seemed like the funniest thing I had ever heard, and we ended up weak with laughter, myself and this nameless neighbour of my sister's – she, in particular, so crippled by mirth you couldn't tell if it was appendicitis or hilarity had her bent over. In the middle of which, she seemed to keel off her chair a little. She rolled to the side, while I just kept looking at her and laughing. Then she hit the ground running and began a low charge, out through the glass door and towards my brother-in-law.

The jet lag hit.

I remember the strangeness of it. This woman lumbering straight at Shay, while he cooked on; the hissing meat, the flames; me thinking, 'Is this night-time? What time is it, anyway?' while the chocolate Rice Krispie cake died on my lips. The woman stooped, as if to tackle Shay by the shins, but when she rose, it was with a small, suddenly buoyant child in her arms, and she was saying, 'Out of there, all right? Out of there!'

The child looked around him, indifferent, more or less,

to this abrupt change of scene. Three, maybe four years old: she set him down on the grass and went to hit him. At least, I thought so. She raised a hand to him and then suddenly back at herself, as though to clear a wasp from in front of her face.

'How many times do I have to tell you?'

Shay lifted an arm to crack a beer, and the child ran off, and the woman just stood there, running her wayward hand through her hair.

That was one thing. There were others. There was Fiona, her cheeks a hectic pink, her eyes suddenly wet from the sheer la-la-lah of pouring wine and laughing gaily and being a beautiful mother forward slash hostess in her beautiful new house.

And there was Conor. My love. Who was late.

It is 2002, and already, none of these people smoke. I sit on my own at the kitchen table and look for someone to talk to. The men in the garden seem no more interesting than they did when I arrived – in their short-sleeved shirts and something about their casual trousers that still screams 'slacks'. I am just back from Australia. I remember the guys you see along Sydney Harbour-front at lunchtime, an endless line of them; running men, tanned and fit; men you could turn around and follow without knowing that you were following them, the same way you might pick up a goddamn Rice Krispie cake and not know that you were eating it, until you spotted the marshmallow on the top.

'Ooh, pink!'

I really want a cigarette now. Fiona's children have never seen one, she told me – Megan burst into tears when an electrician lit up in the house. I pull my bag from the back of the chair and idle my way across the threshold, past Shay, who waves a piece of meat at me, through rain-bleached tricycles and cheerful suburbanites, down to where Fiona's little rowan tree stands tethered to its square stake and the garden turns to mountainside. There is a little log house here for the kids, made out of brown plastic: a bit disgusting actually – the logs look so fake, they might as well be moulded out of chocolate, or some kind of rubberised shit. I lurk behind this yoke – and I am so busy making this seem a respectable thing to do; leaning into the fence, smoothing my skirt, furtively rooting in my bag for smokes, that I do not see him until I light up, so my first sight of Seán (in this, the story I tell myself about Seán) takes place at the beginning of my first exhalation: his body; the figure he makes against the view, made hazy by the smoke of a long-delayed Marlboro Light.

Seán.

He is, for a moment, completely himself. He is about to turn around, but he does not know this yet. He will look around and see me as I see him and, after this, nothing will happen for many years. There is no reason why it should.

It really feels like night-time. The light is wonderful and wrong – it's like I have to pull the whole planet around in my head to get to this garden, and this part of the afternoon and to this man, who is the stranger I sleep beside now.

A WOMAN COMES UP and speaks to him in a low voice. He listens to her over his shoulder, then he twists further to look at a small girl who hangs back from them both.

'Oh for God's sake, Evie,' he says. And he sighs – because

it is not the child herself who is annoying him but something else; something larger and more sad.

The woman goes back to scrub at the gunk on Evie's face with a paper napkin that shreds itself on her sticky skin. Seán watches this for a few seconds. And then he looks over to me.

These things happen all the time. You catch a stranger's eye, for a moment too long, and then you look away.

I was just back from holidays – a week with Conor's sister in Sydney, then north to this amazing place where we learned how to scuba dive. Where we also learned, as I recall, how to have sex while sober; a simple trick, but a good one, it was like taking off an extra skin. Maybe this was why I could meet Seán's eye. I had just been to the other side of the world. I was looking, by my own standards, pretty good. I was in love – properly in love – with a man I would soon decide to marry, so when he looked at me, I did not feel afraid.

Perhaps I should have done.

And I can't, for the life of me, recall what Evie looked like that day. She would have been four, but I can't think how that would play on the girl I know now. All I saw that afternoon was a child with a dirty face. So Evie is just a kind of smudge in the picture, which is otherwise so clear.

Because the amazing thing is how much I got in that first glance: how much, in retrospect, I should have known. It is all there: the twitch of interest I had in Seán, the whole business with Evie; I remember this very clearly, as I remember the neat and indomitable politeness of his wife. I got her straight off, and nothing she subsequently did surprised me or proved me wrong. Aileen, who never changed her hair, who was then and will always remain a size 10. I could wave to Aileen now, across the bridge of years, and she would give me the same look she gave me then, pretty much. Because she knew me too. On sight. And even though she was so smiling and correct, I did not fail to see her intensity.

Aileen, I think it would be fair to say, has not moved on.

I am not sure I have, myself. Somewhere up by the house, Marshmallow Woman is laughing too hard, Conor is elsewhere, Aileen's paper napkin, in a tasteful shade of lime-green, will soon leave shreds of itself on Evie's sticky skin, and Seán will glance my way. But not yet. For the moment, I am just breathing out.

LOVE IS LIKE A CIGARETTE

LET'S START WITH CONOR. Conor is easy. Let's say he has already arrived, that afternoon in Enniskerry. When I go back into the kitchen he is there, lingering and listening, having a good time. Conor is low and burly and, in the summer of 2002, he is my idea of fun.

Conor never takes his jacket off. Under the jacket is a cardigan, then a shirt, then a T-shirt and under that, a tattoo. The wide strap of his bag is slung across his chest, keeping everything tamped down. He is on the mooch. This man never stops checking around him, as though for food. In fact, if he is near food he will be eating it – but neatly, in an intelligent, listening sort of way. His eyes keep travelling the floor and if he looks up it is with great charm: he is caught by something you have said, he thinks you are funny. He might seem preoccupied, but this guy is always ready for a good time.

I loved Conor, so I know what I am talking about here. He comes from a line of shopkeepers and pub owners in Youghal, so he likes to watch people and smile. I used to like this about him. And I liked the bag, it was trendy, and his glasses were trendy too, thick-rimmed and sort of fifties, and he shaved his head, which usually annoyed me but it suited him because his skin was so brown and his skull so sizeable. And his neck was large, and his back bulged and sprouted hair from the shoulders down. What can I say? Sometimes it surprised me that the person I loved was so fantastically male, that the slabs of muscle were covered in slabs of solid fat and the whole of him – all five foot nine, God help us – was fizzed up with hair, so that he became blurred at the edges, when he undressed. No one had told me you could like that sort of thing. But I did.

Conor had just finished a Masters in multimedia, he was a happening geek. I was also in IT, sort of, I work with European companies mainly, on the web. Languages are my thing. Not the romance languages, unfortunately, I do the beer countries, not the wine. Though I still think the umlaut is a really sexy distortion, the way it makes you purse your mouth for it, and all those Scandinavian 'o' and 'u' sounds give me the goose bumps. I went out with a Norwegian guy called Axel once, just to hear him say 'snøord'.

But I went out with Conor for the laugh and I fell in love with him because it was the right thing to do. How could this be possible? That, in all the time I knew him, he never did a cruel thing.

There was no big decision to buy a house, it just made sense. Australia was our last fling, after that everything was salted away for deposits and mortgage insurance and stamp duty and solicitors' fees – Jesus, they wrung us till we squeaked. I can't remember what this did to the love we were supposed to be in. I can't recall the nights. Ours was, anyway, a daytime kind of love; Conor took up windsurfing out at Seapoint, and came back smelling of chips and the sea. On Saturday afternoons we tramped around other people's houses – three-bed semi, Victorian terrace, penthouse flat. We looked at each other standing beside thirties' mantelpieces, and sort of squinted. Or we wandered into separate rooms where we could imagine ourselves in the space more easily, with a wall knocked, or a smell gone, or the place less uninhabited.

We did this for months. We got quite good at it. I could walk into some kip and slap a tobacco-brown leather sofa up against the longest wall, on sight. I could dangle a retro lampshade as soon as you said 'fifties semi', and stick an Eames chair under it, and switch on the light. But I didn't know what my life would be like in that chair, or how I would feel about it. Better, no doubt. I was sure I would feel serious-yet-playful, grown-up and happy, I would be somehow fulfilled. But then again, as I said to Conor.

'Then again.'

There was, when we made love at the end of these long Saturdays, a sense in which we were reclaiming ourselves for ourselves, after some brief theft.

You walk into a stranger's house and it is exciting, that's all, and you are slightly soiled by it. I could feel it, in the second-hand, abandoned kitchens, and in my Sunday-supplement dreams. I could feel it drain away in the moments after waking, when I realised that we hadn't bought, we probably never would buy, a house with a sea view. It didn't seem a lot to ask – a house that would clean your life every time you looked out of it – but it was, apparently. It was far too much to ask. I did the figures up down and sideways and I never could believe the bottom line.

The bottom line was the place we had started out from, before we lost the plot. The bottom line wasn't so much a house as an investment; somewhere to swing our cat, that was not too far out of town.

So we found exactly that; a townhouse in Clonskeagh for three hundred grand. We were the last in, bought off the plans, drank a bottle of Krug to celebrate – all one-hundred-and-twenty euros' worth.

Krug, no less.

It was nice.

I loved Conor then. I really did love him, and all the versions of him I had invented, in those houses, in my head, I loved them all. And I loved some essential thing too; the sense of him I carried around with me, which was confirmed each time I saw him, or a few strange seconds later. We knew each other. Our real life was in some shared head space; our bodies were just the places we used to play. Maybe that's the way lovers should be – not these besotted, fuck-witted strangers that are myself and Seán, these actors in a bare room.

Anyway. Before our lives became a desolation of boredom, rage and betrayal, I loved Seán. I mean, Conor.

Before our lives became a desolation of boredom, rage and all the rest of it, I loved Conor Shiels, whose heart was steady, and whose body was so solid and warm.

The weekend after contracts were exchanged, we went into the unfinished house and looked around. Then we sat on the concrete floor and held hands.

'Listen,' he said.

'What?'

'Listen to the money.'

The place was going up by seventy-five euro a day, he said, which was – he did the calculations under flickering eyelids – about five cents a minute. Which didn't seem like much, I thought. Which seemed almost piffling, after all we had been through. Still, you could almost feel it, a pushing in the walls; the toaster would pop out fivers, the wood of the new-laid floors would squeeze out paper money and start to flower.

And, for some reason, we were terrified.

Don't tell me otherwise.

The house fitted Lego-like with its neighbour, which had the basement and split the middle floor, and this threw me a bit, the fact that it was only half a house until you went upstairs. It was like the place had suffered a stroke.

Not that this was a problem, or at least not a problem you could identify. I just hadn't expected it. And I still dream about this house, about walking up those steps and opening the front door.

The day we moved in, Conor was inside in among the boxes, sitting at his laptop like a demented organist, cursing the internet connection. I didn't complain. We needed the money. The next few months were all about work and there was something frantic and lonely about our love in that little house (don't get sentimental, I tell myself, the sockets moved in the wall every time you stuck in a plug). We clung to each other. Six months, nine – I don't know how long that phase lasted. Mortgage love. Shagging at 5.3 per cent. Until one day we decided to take out a couple of car loans and get married on the money instead.

Vroom vroom.

It was the silliest thing we had ever done – either of us – and it was surprisingly good fun. It happened, after much fuss and diplomatic incident, on a lovely day in April; church, hotel, bouquet, the lot.

ABOUT SEVEN HUNDRED OF CONOR'S COUSINS came up from Youghal. I'd never seen anything like it: the way they stood their rounds of drink, fixed their little hats in the mirrors, and checked the weight of the hotel cutlery when they picked it up to eat. They treated the day like a professional engagement, and danced until three. Conor said it might as well be your funeral; he said they hunt in packs. And my mother – who had, it turned out, 'always been saving for this day' – led a seasoned troupe of the Dublin middle classes, many of them old, all of them entirely happy, as they chatted and sat and sipped their peculiar drinks: Campari, whiskey and red, Harvey's Bristol Cream. We were just the excuse. We knew it, as we went upstairs to change out of our duds and ride each other rotten against the back of the bedroom door. We were beside the point. Free.

My mother is there in the photograph album (five hundred euro, bound in cream leather, now mouldering under the kitchen counter in Clonskeagh). She wore a lilac-grey suit and a fascinator, no less, in grey and mauve, complete with face net, and those funny black feathers that arc out, stripped to bobbing dots of black. She is there beside me. Tiny. Her hair a kind of mystery; she had it caught up some way at the back.

My mother's favourite film was *Brief Encounter*, she knew how to cry under a veil. And she always spent money on her hair. Even when she was skint, she had a way of convincing people to make her look beautiful, that it would be possible, and they did their best by her. When it comes to the hairdresser's, she used to say, it pays to leave your moods at home.

She wouldn't give me away, refused point blank, fixed me up instead with my father's brother; a man I had not seen since I was thirteen years old. I thought we might meet the day before, at least, but he turned up on the morning, fresh from the airport, and when everyone went off in the first car, we were left in the front room looking at each other, while the driver idled outside.

It was the strangest moment of a very strange day. I stood trembling at the window, in my pewter silk Alberta Ferretti with a mad Philip Treacy yoke (you might even call it a fascinator) stuck to the side of my head, and every time I made to move, this guy checked his fat watch and said:

'Make them wait. You're the bride.'

Finally, at some mysteriously ordained moment, he crossed the living room carpet, took me by the shoulders, and said, 'You know who it is you remind me of? My own mother. You have her lovely eyes.'

Then he offered me an old-fashioned arm and conducted me out to the car.

Was that the creepiest bit? Taking the slow march down the aisle on the arm of this old geezer, who hadn't expressed an emotion, by the look of him, since 1965? I don't know. The local church, which does a good line in cherry blossom, also has a very peculiar crucifix suspended over the altar. A huge thing, made of wood. The figure of Christ, which isn't especially gory, hangs not just on the front, but also on the back of it – this for the people who end up on the other side of the altar. And it distracted me throughout the ceremony, the way it used to distract me as a child, this double Jesus, back to back with His own reflection. Standing there, in two-hundred-and-twenty euros' worth of underwear, never mind the dress, I wanted to say, 'What were they thinking?' This just a milder version of the things that used to flash through my head in this church – the shapeless obscenities that plagued my school years, and which started, at a guess, at my father's funeral when I was thirteen. All grown-up, I stood where his coffin once lay (his ghost drifted, head first, through the small of my back), and I regretted my choice of basque over Spanx, while the priest said:

Do you take?

And I said:

Yes. Yes, I do.

And Conor smiled.

Outside, the sun shone and the photographer waved, while the shiny black cars nudged each other in the yard.

We had a great time. The seven hundred cousins from Youghal, and my uncle in from Brussels. We had, Conor and myself, enormous amounts of sex on the strength of it, and a holiday in Croatia (cheap after all that excess), and we woke up back in Clonskeagh one morning; hungover, giddy and unafraid.

The next year, the next two years, I was as happy as I have ever been.

I know this. Despite the bitterness that was to follow, I know that I was happy. We worked like crazy and partied when we could. We fell into bed, most nights, after a hard day and a quick knock-back of whatever: I was beyond Chardonnay by then – let's call them the Sauvignon Blanc years.

Conor had a sudden jump of money when he hooked a travel company who wanted to get online. He was working with other people by then, you might even say he was working *for* other people, but I don't know if he cared. The internet was made for Conor: the way he was always interested but could never settle on any one thing. He spent hours – days – at the screen, then he was up and out of the chair; walking into town; cycling over to the Forty Foot where he swam, in cold seas and warm, with much splashing and whooshing. Everything was slightly too much, with Conor. He wore too many clothes, and when he was naked he heaved large sighs and rubbed his chest, and farted hugely as he stood in the bathroom to pee. And I ended up not believing it, somehow. I ended up – this seems a peculiar thing to say – not believing a single thing he did; thinking it was all gesture and expostulation, it was all air.

SUNNY AFTERNOON

BUT THIS WAS LATER. Or perhaps it had happened already, perhaps it was happening all along. We might have run along these parallel tracks, of believing and not believing, for the rest of our lives. I don't know.

Because we were also flying along, myself and Conor, we were happily, sensibly, married married married. The next time I saw Seán, I had forgotten all about him. It was 2005. We were stuck at home for another summer, clearing the costs of buying the house, so we went down to Brittas Bay one bank holiday Monday, to see Fiona.

She was there for four or five weeks with the kids while Shay came down when he could – which was to say, when it suited him. You have to understand that Shay was coining it at the time, so not only did they have a house practically in the country, which is to say in Enniskerry, but a few miles away, thirty minutes in the car, they had a site in a posh mobile home park by the sea. This was – I don't know – a hundred, two hundred grand's worth of tat on a caravan site by the beach. It is not something I would normally be jealous of, except that I didn't have two hundred grand to throw around like that, and nothing makes you jealous like something you didn't actually want in the first place.

We got up early and drove down the N11, Conor with his windsurfing gear, and me with a couple of bottles of red and a load of steaks I grabbed for the barbecue. I offered the meat to Fiona when we arrived; a bulging white plastic bag that was stained on the inside with blood turning brown.

'Ooh!' she said.

'It seemed like a good idea, in the shop.'

'It was a good idea,' she said. 'What is it?'

'It's an arse in a bag,' said Conor. Which was exactly what it looked like, dangling there.

'Leg of lamb steaks,' I said.

My niece, Megan, started to laugh. She must have been nearly eight, and Jack, her little brother who was five, ran in shouting circles. Conor went after him, hunched over with hands waggling, until he caught the child, and threw him on the ground screaming, while Conor went (something like), 'Har har, I am the arse, har har.'

I thought Jack was going to vomit, that this would be the end of us as a Happy Bank Holiday Family, but Fiona just gave the pair of them a steady look, then said, 'I hope I have room,' before clumping up the little wooden steps and going into the caravan.

When I followed, she was on her knees, pushing the meat like a pillow into the bottom drawer of the fridge. There was a pile of salad and vegetables beside her on the floor.

'God, this place.'

'It's lovely,' I said.

'Bedsit *sur mer*.'

'Well,' I said – because it was hard to know what to do with it. I looked around. The plastic partitions had a sort of inbuilt wallpaper pattern, and everything shook a bit when you walked. But it was nice, too. A toy house.

'The woman three down has wooden blinds.'

'It's not supposed to be real,' I said.

'Oh, you have No Idea,' she said.

Shay, it turned out, was thinking about a proper summer house near Gorey, or they might look on the Continent, probably France. This Fiona said later, after too much sun and wine, when there were more people to hear. But in the morning, kneeling in front of the little fridge on a floor made slithery with sand, I felt sorry for her, my so-pretty sister, who would always be outdone by the woman three caravans down.

The weather improved through the day. The clouds headed out to sea and their shadows moved, sombre and precise, over the water. It was better than the telly. We sat outside in our big sunglasses, and waggled our painted toes, turquoise and navy blue. Fantastic. I should have brought our mother along, she would have liked it, but it hadn't occurred to me. I don't know why.

Conor was out on the central green, throwing frisbee for the kids, treating them like dogs.

'Fetch!' he shouted. 'Fetch!'

'They're not dogs, Conor,' I said, as the children stuck their faces in the grass and tried to lift the frisbee with their teeth.

'Sit!' shouted Conor. 'Paw!'

It wasn't the children I was worried about, it was their mother. But she gave another of her measured looks and said, 'Good ploy.'

There was some code of practice here, and I never quite knew what it was.

Another child arrived. She and Megan jigged briefly in front of each other, then she too ran after the frisbee, over and back, jumping up in a doomed sort of way.

'No, here. No here. No give it to me.'

And she tripped on her flowery flip-flops and cried. Or yowled, actually. It was an interesting noise, even in the open air. It cut out as she stopped to inhale (or choke, perhaps), then it started again, even shriller than before.

Conor, to be fair to him, did not run over to tickle her while har-harring about arse. This was a substantial child, both round and tall, and it was hard to put an age on her. It was hard to know if those were small breasts or largish amounts of fat under the cross-over cardigan – the very pinkness of which insisted she was still a child.

A woman walked across the grass and spoke to her quietly, then waited and spoke again. Which only made things worse, as far as I could tell. Megan and Jack looked on, in a state of uneasy, furtive delight. They loved a crisis, that pair. Made them shiver. Which, in turn, made me wonder how much shouting and mayhem they saw at home.

Fiona was half-out of her chair, but she seemed unsure. Even the child's father hung back. They had been on their way from the car park when she ran ahead and he stood apart, waiting for the fit to subside. I remember feeling that someone should be grown-up about this; effect introductions, offer drinks. So I waved. And he shrugged and came over, and for a moment, it seemed as though the rest of the world had gone into slow motion, leaving us outside and free.

It was Seán. Of course. More handsome than I remembered, with a tan and longer, curly hair. A bit cheeky, actually, from the front; a bit too ironical. As though he knew me, which, I was keen to tell him, he did not. Or not yet. So we had got to, 'Your point being?' before the seat of his trousers had touched the stripy cotton of the fold-up chair.

I am surprised, as I remember all this – the immediacy of it, the copulatory crackle in the air – that it took almost another year before we did the bold thing; before we pulled the houses down around us; the townhouse and the cottage and the semi-d. All those mortgages. Pulled the sky down too, to settle over us like a cloth.

Blackout.

Or maybe he was like that with all the girls.

I have to backtrack a little, and say that there were other things that could have happened with our lives. We might have done it all in secret, either. I mean, no one had to know.

But, back in the daylight of the caravan park, Evie was still baying, Aileen was murmuring in a firm and even tone, while Fiona turned to Seán, like a fool, and said, 'Would she like an ice-pop, d'you think?'

Seán winced. Our children, whose selective hearing could beat bats', came running across the grass, and Evie limped after, whinging in a half-hearted and hopeful sort of way.

'I'm afraid Evie doesn't eat ice-pops,' said Seán. 'Do you,

Evie?' She stopped, her flip-flops clutched to her chest, and after a long and horrible pause said, 'No.'

He sat with her in his arms during the wrangle that followed, which ended with Megan and Jack banished to the other side of the mobile home to eat their half-promised ice-pops, out of sight. He is a small enough man, Seán. He rocked her, this large child, through distant and imagined slurps and suckings – I wanted a damn ice-pop myself by this stage – while Fiona talked to Aileen about minders and crèche fees, and I thought, Wouldn't it be better just to hit the child? Wouldn't it be quicker and more humane?

I exaggerate. Of course.

Evie was a normal enough eight-year-old girl, Aileen was not a monster of calm, Seán was a businessman with too sharp a crease in his summer pants. It was a boring, nice day. After lunch, Conor pulled his hat down over his face and pulled his T-shirt up to warm his brown and hairy belly in the sun. I folded a sheet of paper, the way we used to at school, so you could open and shut it like a little bird's beak with fingers and thumbs, first forward, then out to the side, and myself and Megan played fortunes: Go Figure, You Smell, Easy Peasy, with True Love hidden under the last flap. After lengthy negotiations, Evie and Jack went inside to watch a DVD. They did not have the resources, it seemed, to do anything else.

In the middle of the afternoon, my brother-in-law Shay turned up. He stopped on the grass, held his phone up high and, with a cartoonish finger, turned it off. Then he came on to the deck, kissed Fiona and said hello all round. Then he walked inside and switched off the television, and told everyone to get down to the beach, with much shouting for togs and towels and inflatable toys while Fiona found – or couldn't find – missing sandals and keys to the front door and the hundred mysterious objects her children need: water, suncream, a green golfing visor that Megan liked, Jack's yellow plastic rake; because, as far as I can see, kids will do anything to stay in a place where they are happy enough, up to and including making their mother weep.

'Have you ever heard of a Loon A Tic asylum?' I said to Megan, who regarded me with wise, monkey eyes. Meanwhile Seán's wife, Aileen, just read the paper until everyone was ready, then she walked back to their car and lifted a single bag from the boot.

'Right!' she said. 'Onward!'

CONOR LAUGHED all the way home.

'The ice-pop!' he said. 'The fucking ice-pop!'

And I intoned, 'Evie doesn't eat ice-pops, do you Evie?'

'Jesus Christ.'

'Apparently she has some kind of thing. The child,' I said, because that was what Fiona muttered to me by the sink, as we washed up.

'Like what?'

'You know, something wrong. Fiona didn't say.'

Evie was a funny, disturbed little article, there was no doubt about it. She didn't seem the same age or stage as Megan, though they were both around eight years old – or maybe I was biased, my niece being such a little sprite. If I had known more about these things I might have put her on a spectrum, or tried to. Except that Evie was all there – alert, trembling with it –

she just found things very difficult. And whether this was, as I suspected, her mother's fault, I couldn't say for sure. I did find her slightly unbearable, though. It might have been something to do with the fat; those plump, kissable baby wrists; but with the wrong sort of face above them, the wrong kind of eyes. I didn't say this to Conor, of course. I mean, I might have said, 'She is quite an object,' but I am pretty sure I didn't say the fat made her unpleasant to me; I did not share my 'failure to love', as Megan's teacher calls a sin these days. Besides, whatever slight annoyance ran through me when I looked at Evie left, as a residue, something both calm and keen.

Pity.

'Poor child,' I said. 'It's all her, you know,' meaning the mother. And Conor said, 'They should both be shot.'

He seemed to like them well enough at the time. He chatted to Seán as we all trekked over to the cold Irish Sea and Fiona chased and cajoled her children into their togs and creams, while Shay opened a bottle of red, sat on the rug and shut down, massively and at speed – it was frightening to watch – like a power cut running through Manhattan.

'I thought he looked terrible,' I said to Conor in the car.

'Who?'

'My brother-in-law,' I said. 'I thought he looked like shite.'

'Shay's all right,' he said. 'Don't you worry about Shay.'

Conor was being a bit obtuse, these days. He was recently finding the whole contraception thing a bit 'unconducive', for example. To what? He did not say.

We did not talk about Seán, as far as I recall. Perhaps there was no need to. It is possible that we held an uncomplicated silence, the rest of the way home.

Certainly, in his togs, Seán – my downfall, my destiny – cut a less than imposing figure. I suppose you could say that of us all. In the bare sunshine we looked a bit peeled. Fiona, being, in her day, the most beautiful girl in Terenure, didn't bare an inch, of course. She had some way with sarong and towel that made Brittas look like Cannes, and when we toyed with the idea of a swim, said, 'Oh, I was in this morning,' because whatever effort she puts into it all (and I suspect it is considerable) she never lets on.

So it was just the four of us, Conor and me, Seán and Aileen, playing Houdini with bra straps and towels, then pretending not to look at each other's bodies on the beach. Truth be told, I didn't really bother with Seán that day, I was too busy checking out his wife; so dull when dressed, so elegant and boyish in the nip, never mind her age. Her odd little breasts screamed 'breasts' at you, though – they looked so tender on her little bony ribs, like they had been grown there specially.

Seán gave me the full flat of his face, as if to ask if I had some problem with the body of his wife. But I had no problem with it, why should I? I had problems enough of my own. I had to keep Conor in front of me, for a start, until the other pair were safely wet, or, at least, looking the other way.

'What is it?' said Conor. 'What do you want?'

While I hung on to him, bickering and talking rubbish, managing the towel.

Seán headed down to the surf, hugging himself, with

high shoulders and picking, bouncy feet. Aileen gave the sea a cold look, snapped her suit down under her bum and started to walk. Then, at the last moment, Evie flung herself in the sand and caught her mother's leg, hugging her thigh in terrible supplication.

'Evie, please stop that.'

While my sister checked round her with vague eyes and loudly said, 'Megan, what did you do to Evie?'

And I walked away from them in silence, and kept walking until the water covered my thighs.

Then I screamed.

'Whuu! Freezing!'

But it pulled all the uncertainty out of my bones – the surprise of lifting your feet and finding there was no need for sand. I made my way through the wave's sharp swell, towards the flat line of the horizon. By the time I turned back to the shore, pushed and loved by all that weight of water, I was happy.

I watched from the sea as Aileen straggled up the beach to tend to Evie, and I realised that her thin body wasn't fit, it was just busy. You could see it in the hunch of her shoulders; how she might walk at speed, but she took no pleasure in it.

Conor would stay in the water for another twenty minutes, his windsurf board forgotten on the roof of the car. Shay, meanwhile, had fallen backwards on the lime-green, polka-dot rug, belly to the sky. Which left Seán, and Seán's lacklustre desiring – because we all wanted him to want us. At least I think we did, disporting ourselves (isn't that the word?) about the place where he sat, our bodies shocked into delight by the cold sea. There we were: Fiona, who was a sort of dream, and his wife who did not matter, and me, who was – for these few moments at least – the bouncing girl. As I came up the short slope of the beach, and bent for my towel, and flung my hair back and said, 'Hooo-eeee!' I was the girl who liked it. The fat one.

I was the nightmare.

Or I felt like the nightmare. It must have been the way he looked at me.

This tiny drama happened and then disappeared immediately, as if by arrangement, and we sat around on a spoiled patchwork of towels, as though used to pretending that everyone was fully dressed. We talked about the year we realised you could have more than one bathing suit – which, in my case, was the year in question, when I had to go up a size, due to too much wedded bliss, and went mad in the shop and bought two. 'One on, one drying on the line.'

Seán talked about wearing his father's navy underpants on the beach in Courtown, and never forgiving his mother for it, the way she stitched up the flies and said they were just like the real thing. The story made us realise how much older he was than us – which also explained the stone house down the road from Fiona and Shay's in Enniskerry. Myself and Conor still got age-rage when people waggled their bricks and mortar at us. 'You have a nice house? That's because you're old, you bastard,' though Seán – so wiry and compact – seemed hardly grown-up at all. The pair of them, husband and wife, were like mantelpiece ornaments, each so particular in the way they moved, and I felt myself inflate slowly on the beach beside them. I was huge! I was horny! I was . . . careful. When I looked at Seán, and he at me, it was always eye to eye.

In fact, as I discovered later, Seán wasn't judging my body one way or another. He just waited for my own judgement to rise and then smiled it back at me. It was one of his tricks. I should have known about his tricks.

Two passing teenagers, for example, fabulous and tall; he stared at them for a second too long – stared hard, like he might have to go over there and fuck them, right now. Then he turned back to look at disappointing you.

I was sort of scorched by it, I have to say.

This is why Fiona started burbling on about buying a house in France. It was because she wanted to impress Seán – a man who, in his Speedos, was not exactly a siren song. He stirred us up. Everything he said was funny, and everything seemed to do you down. Or buoy you up. He could do that too. He sat about; a black T-shirt covering his little mound of stomach, and he pushed into the sand with his tough, white toes.

Even in the strong sun, I was caught by the beauty of his eyes, which were larger than a man's eyes should be and more easily hurt. I saw the child in him that afternoon, it was easy to see: an eight-year-old charmer, full of mischief and swagger. But I don't know if I saw how tactical it all was. I don't think I saw the way he was threatened by his own desires, or how jealousy and desire ran so close in him he had to demean a little the thing he wanted. For example, me.

Or not me. It was hard to tell.

One way or another, we all ended up boasting. Practically naked as we were, in our very ordinary, Irish bodies (except

Fiona's, which wasn't on show), we sat and bragged for a while, while the children dug in the sand and ran about, and the beach and the sky continued, beautiful, without us.

'What was all that about?' said Conor, in the car on the way home. 'Jesus.'

WILL YOU LOVE ME TOMORROW

THAT WINTER, JOAN COMPLAINED of swelling in her feet, which, for our mother, was a terrible comedown, the row of shoes she had, going back thirty years, all forsworn for Granny boots: she just hated it. She got supplements in the health food shop and complained of depression – she was, actually, depressed, I thought – and it never occurred to her, or to any of us, to do anything about it except mope and talk on the phone about kitten heels and peppermint lotion and the various shades in which you might get support tights.

And I had gone back on the pill, which isn't exactly important, except that the pill always makes *me* depressed: foggy and guilty and permanently just that tiny bit swollen, so the surface of me is too needy and stupid, somehow. I am not explaining it very well. I just think that if I hadn't been on the pill things would have gone differently; I might have been able to listen better to my mother on the phone, or think better, but it was like I had gone to the edges of myself, and what was in the centre was anyone's guess. Nothing, that is one answer. Or nothing much.

And I was busy, it seemed like I was always on a plane. There were times my toiletries never made it out of their see-through plastic bag.

Conor's mother arrived for the weekend; she sat there eating breakfast and floated the opinion that two pillowcases were more hygienic, she always thought, than just one.

'Sleep,' she said. 'It's a third of your life.' And I didn't throw her out or shout at her that the son she reared didn't know you could change sheets, he thought they came with the bed.

'You know,' I said. 'That makes a lot of sense.'

Mrs Shiels had five children: two in Youghal, and two breeding mightily in Dundrum and Bondi. A capable, glamorous woman, she was all set to use us for her Dublin shopping base – she knew it and I knew it. For Christmas, I got her some vouchers for a posh hotel.

'The Merrion!' she said. 'Lovely.'

This was a Christmas I could have been with my own mother, but which I spent instead in the middle of a scrummage down in Youghal, with forty people whose names I did not know, each and every one of whom hated Dubliners (don't tell me otherwise) for the fact that they weren't from fucking Youghal.

Christ.

I can't believe I am free of all that. I just can't believe it. That all you have to do is sleep with somebody and get caught and you never have to see your in-laws again. Ever. Pfffft! Gone. It's the nearest thing to magic I have yet found.

But the pill is important for another reason too, I suppose, because if it hadn't been for the pill, I might not have slept with Seán that time in Montreux. Which was – and this is a peculiar thing to say – the only time it did not matter. Apart from anything else, there was a lot of, I think, Alsace Riesling involved.

It happened at a conference. Of course. A week of management-speak on a Swiss lake with flow charts and fondue, and a little trip on a wooden boat, with a mixed gang of semi-state and private sector, a few from Galway, most Dublin-based, and drinking on the last couple of nights, until 4 a.m. Most of them, I might also mention, were men.

The title of the week was 'Beyond the EU'. I was there to talk 'International Internet Strategy' – delighted to get the invite, which was a step up for me. The hotel was a confection in cream and red velvet, with gilt everywhere and stains on the carpets that might have been a hundred years old. And there on the first morning, under the heading 'The Culture of Money' was the name 'Seán Vallely'.

'You made it,' he said. He looked better than I remembered. Maybe it was the fact that he was dressed.

'I wondered who it was,' I said.

'Ah, wheels within wheels,' he said.

We shook hands.

His palm felt old, I thought, but most palms do.

I checked him out giving a seminar that first morning: I glanced in through the open door and saw him eating the room. His open jacket flapped behind him, as he turned to one corner and then the other. He worked the air in front of his chest; he cupped the thought, and held it out, and let it go.

'Why,' he said, 'do you dislike rich people?'

It was quite a spiel.

'You. What's your name? Billy. OK, Billy. Do you like rich people?'

'I'm not bothered.'

'You take it personally, don't you? The house, the car, the holidays in the sun. You take it personally, because you're Irish. If you were American, you'd let them have it. Because, you know, these people are not connected to you. They bought their nice house and your name didn't even come up. They went to the Bahamas and they didn't even forget to invite you.'

There were two speakers each morning, and people were split into groups for workshops during the afternoons. I thought Seán was sleeping with the 'Global Tax' woman, or that he had slept with her. But, I learned later, they just didn't like each other, or so he said.

Meanwhile there were the chocolate tastings and shopping opportunities and much rubbish to talk. The wilder ones, myself included, formed a kind of gang, with large amounts of drinking to get through. There were two Northern Irish guys 'from either side of the divide' whose catchphrase became, 'just so long as nobody gets shot'. There was a really nice gay guy who played torch songs at the piano in the bar and the Global Tax woman, who drove me up the wall by stopping the conversation, many times, in order to make her point yet more clear. By Wednesday night it was a drinking competition, and I had her knocked out by the fourth round. On Thursday I ended up in one of the Northerners' rooms, polishing off the mini-bar with the other Northern guy and Seán; the queen of international tax returns passed out on the second bed. On the last night – Friday – Seán met me on my way back from the ladies, and he turned to gather me up, saying, 'Come here. I have something to show you.' At least I think that is what he said. I may not remember the words exactly, but I remember his hand on the small of my back, and I remember knowing what we were about to do. It seemed that choice had nothing to do with it, or that I had chosen a long time ago. Not him, necessarily, but this; waiting for the lift in sudden silence with a man who did not even bother to court me. Or had that happened already? Maybe he would court me later. Things, clearly, did not happen in a particular order anymore: first this, and then that. First a kiss, and then bed. Maybe it was the drink, but my sense of time was undone, as idly as a set of shoelaces, that you do not notice until you look down.

In the lift we made small-talk. Don't ask me what about.

A part of me said that there would be other people in his room, like the previous night's fun – that we were still a happy bunch of people who were trying to move beyond the EU – another part surely hoped that there wouldn't be. But there is little point in agonising over something so simple. We went upstairs to have sex. And it seemed like a great idea at the time. I was, besides, so drunk, I only remember it in patches.

We had an amazing session outside the room, I do remember that; as I resisted going in the door and he turned back to persuade me. My memory skips the beginning of it, like a needle in an old record, so I have lost the moment of decision, the leaning in. But I remember how he slayed me with kisses, how, when I struggled to open my eyes, I was surprised to find the hotel corridor still there; the dizzy carpet, the receding line of identical doors, and the wallpaper, in vertical stripes of scarlet flock. As I continued to leave and he continued to keep me, the kiss was a sweet argument and pursuit, so tranced and articulate, his left hand on my arm, the other holding his plastic door key, not yet slipped home.

It was the luxury of the kiss that held me, the pure pointless, greedy delight. Even when the lock whirred and the door clicked open, we carried on, and it was only the sound of people coming out of the lift that sent us scurrying inside, laughing in the darkness.

After the kiss – the five-minute, ten-minute, two-hour kiss – the actual sex was a bit too actual, if you know what I mean. There is another blank when I try to recall how we got from the door to the bed, after which, much enthusiastic bouncing and writhing, despite the fact that I couldn't really feel much, I don't think, and Seán (who is now the love of my life – my goodness, how it betrays him to say this), took about half an hour to come.

At the time, I thought it was the drink that slowed him down. But Seán only ever pretends to drink. Now I know him better; that inward look as he tries to catch his pleasure, the thing that puts him off his stroke, I realise, is age. Or the fear of age.

As if I cared about his age.

Or perhaps this is not how it was in Montreux. I might be imposing the lover I know now on the memory of the man I slept with then. He might have been, that first time, thrilling and keen, pitch perfect; the impulse inseparable from the action. Maybe that is what first times are for.

All I know is that one night, on the shores of Lake Geneva, in a small room among other small rooms, in the middle of Seán's long effort, I turned my head to see his keys and loose change on the bedside locker; beyond them the open door of the bathroom where the fan still droned, and I remembered who I was.

I don't know if Seán was surprised how quickly I left afterwards, but he was practically asleep and did not detain me. The last thing I remember was the door at my back and the long corridor stretching out on either side of me. I think I got lost. I have some idea that I tried – quite hard – to get into my room, but it was on the wrong floor: the numbers had confused me. I lurched through the carpeted corridors and got into lifts and out again, and I met no one, or maybe just one couple, who said nothing but stood in by the wall as I passed. But even this is not clear. Some shutter came down, and it did not rise until I woke the next day, safe in my own bed, half-undressed, with all the lights ablaze.

It maddened me. I did not feel guilty, exactly, but I did feel a little mad, I think. I couldn't face the breakfast room, for a start. I put my sunglasses on and headed to a local patisserie, then I took my hangover to the railway station, and I got the first train out of there, a neat, old-fashioned little thing, with bench seats, which went a surprising distance up into the mountains, through tunnels and hidden passes, until it emerged into high meadow lands strewn with Alpine flowers and grazed by chocolate-bar cows with bells around their beautiful, pendulous, mauve necks. The few scattered houses had heart-shapes cut out of their wooden balconies, and white quilts thrown over the rails to air in the sun. And it was all so wonderful and silly, I decided to get out at Gstaad, which turned out to be a village of a few streets, with twee little shops, all with names like Rolex or Cartier. There was a Gucci shop and a Benetton shop and a delicatessen full of astonishing cheese. I walked the entire village, and there wasn't a single place where you could buy cornflakes, or muesli, or even toilet paper and I wondered, did the rich people get these things flown in? Perhaps they did not need them: they had moved beyond.

My adultery – I didn't know what else to call it – lingered in my bones; a slight ache as I walked, the occasional, disturbing trace of must. I had showered that morning, but I realised I would have to go back and clean up again, and the thought made me laugh out loud. It was a vaguely horrified laugh, but still. I did not feel guilty, that afternoon in Gstaad, I felt suicidal. Or the flip side of suicidal: I felt like I had killed my life, and no one was dead. On the contrary, we were all twice as alive.

I also felt, as I went to pack and face the dreaded Seán, that the whole business was a little disappointing, let's face it – as seismic moral shifts go. In the foyer, and on the minibus to the airport, he ignored me so strenuously I felt like writing him a note. 'What makes you think I might care?' It was hardly worth mentioning; not to Seán and certainly not to Conor. And though this seems hard to believe, I returned to my Dublin life as though nothing had happened; as though the lake, the mountains, the whole of Switzerland, was a lie someone had told, to keep the rest of the world amused.

TOORA LOORA LOORA

HINDSIGHT IS A WONDERFUL THING. With hindsight it was clear there was something wrong with Joan long before my hotel encounter, that she hadn't been entirely right for some time. But there were so many reasons we could not see it, not least of which was that she did not want us to.

Our mother was a great beauty, in her day. Appearances were important to her. And because she was, in a way, too beautiful, she worked hard to keep the show on the road. She loved to be normal; to chat and to charm. When she was 'on', she lit up the room.

I used to be jealous of those strangers, who looked at my mother and loved her for half an hour at a time. Sometimes, it seemed as though we only got the downside: the despair in front of the open wardrobe door, the loneliness when there was no one there to admire. There were times, on the phone, when you could hear the drag in her voice; a loss of belief, as though there might be no one listening on the other end of the line.

I didn't get my mother's looks, but I got some of that thing she had, the lift as you walk into a crowded room. I got some of her chat too, her addiction to the phone. And her avoidance of the phone. There were days she let it ring out, for reasons too painful and absurd to explain. It always worked both ways for Joan. Her pleasures were too deep; she had to manage them constantly. So she always looked 'a fright' or 'fine', which is to say, perfect. And she was tough as hell on the rest of the world. Ruthless. What worked, what didn't – hundreds of rules about foundation, lipstick, about whether to conceal or reveal: arms over forty, shoulders over fifty, the lines on your neck. Illness was not something she allowed herself. It was so unattractive. And terribly hard on the skin.

My mother lived forever, every time you looked at her, and she smoked like Hedy Lamarr. She was the last smoker in Dublin. She snuck out into the garden to do it, so her grandchildren would not cry.

She was at it again, at Megan's next birthday in Enniskerry. You would look around and find her gone, then just as mysteriously back again. Megan was nine, so this party was a much more civilised affair, with friends from school and parents who dropped them at the kerb. It was amazing how much had changed. Out the back, the rowan tree was a sturdy, tall thing, and the fence had been rebuilt, to hide the new houses that now blocked their little slice of view. Shay threatened to arrive home and then did not, so it was just myself and Fiona and our mother, and it seemed a long time since we had played at being couples around Fiona's witty formica table, with the men outside, checking the sky for rain. There was no wine. We wandered about, cooking ready-made lasagne and drinking tea, while a tight little herd of nine-year-old girls thundered about the house, trailed by one forlorn little brother.

Joan complained of being tired, took off her too-tight shoes, and fell asleep in an armchair. When she woke, she was agitated by the fact she had nodded off.

'Did I say anything?' then laughed at herself for her consternation.

She was right not to trust us. I had taken a photo of her, a secret one, 'My mother, asleep'. I could not help myself.

I was worried sometimes by the fact that she was on her own in Terenure, we all were – her battalions of friends and lost causes notwithstanding – but our mother did not look lonely in her sleep, even though she was, in a way, 'alone'. She looked like someone who is loved.

I might be biased. The picture looms on my screensaver and then cross fades but it is never as lovely as I remember her, that day. The older you get the less you dream they say but, absent as she was and utterly still, my mother looked, by some indistinguishable sweetness, very much alive.

And young. She was fifty-nine years old.

When she woke up, all fussed, we laughed and told her she had snored. Then Jack was sent upstairs for saying, 'Granny farted in her sleep. Granny farted.'

'You always have to push it,' shouted Fiona at his busy little legs as they disappeared above her, while Joan, who was genuinely shocked as well as amused, said, 'It's only harmless. Would you leave the child.'

I had a mild interest in Evie that day – seeing as I had slept with her father, don't you know – but I couldn't figure out which one she was. The girls Megan had invited were ridiculously large and hard to fathom. They wore oversized party dresses, or funky tops; two at least were in tracksuit bottoms – you couldn't even tell who they thought they were. These people had, besides, no interest in us, they had each other to love; the way they looked at each other was so passionate and shy.

I set out the plates with the real linen napkins that Fiona handed me, and the real glasses and metal cutlery. I put a jug of sparkling water on the table and another of orange juice; all of which I thought silly. These were big, uncomfortable children, not grown-ups – throw a bag of tortilla chips at them, I thought, and retire.

'Who wants lasagne?'

One girl, a tall, soft creature called Saoirse, raised her hand. She was stuffed into a pink satin dress that a five-year-old might choose, and under her arm was a haze of golden-red hair.

I glanced at Fiona. She rolled her eyes in dread.

These children weren't growing, so much as being replaced.

'Come and eat!'

It troubled me quite a bit, actually – the hair. It looked beautiful, when it should have been disgusting. And it was twice as disgusting as it should have been, when you looked up from it to the big pudding-face of the child. I should get out more, I thought – this can not be as strange as I think it is. And I also thought, *Something has gone wrong.*

Then I saw Evie. She revealed herself with a flash of her father's too-beautiful eyes. It happened when she looked straight at me, like the opening of a hidden door. She was still a bit puppyish around the chest, but the fat was mostly gone.

And something else had changed – I mean, apart from everything, because everything had changed – but something essential had shifted. She looked happy. Or not happy so much as connected, for once. Not so scared.

It made me uneasy, the idea that she used to be afraid. I wondered what kind of man I had slept with – how many months ago now? – and would he arrive in through the door. Three months. It was three months since Montreux and I never wanted to lay eyes on Seán Vallely again. I wasn't just mortified, I was actually averse; the thought of speaking to him was slightly soiling, like putting on used clothes after you've had a shower.

Even so, I was caught by his daughter. I watched her, as though she might hold some key to this man, whose eyes seemed to make more sense on her face than they did on his own; the long black lashes just the same, the same sea-grey with a pale sunburst around the pupil, of white or gold.

I had nothing to say to her.

'Would you like some juice?' I asked, as the girls gathered round the table for lasagne and coleslaw – not a pink marshmallow in sight.

'Yes please.'

'Oh look at that great hair,' I touched her black curls, which pleased her. 'Do you dry it yourself?'

She was moist with sweat. They all were.

'Sometimes,' she said.

'Or your Mum?'

'If I got straightener, it would be all the way down my back.'

'Well,' I said. By which I meant, 'Time enough.'

'Sometimes my Dad does it,' she said. But this was too intimate for me, and I had to move away.

After the cake and candles, I took out my iPod and found myself in the middle of a sudden clamour of tweenies, demanding Justin Timberlake.

'Hang on,' I said, and obliged the white bud of the earpiece into Evie's ear. As soon as the music came through, they ran off, grabbing for the other earpiece, switching tracks, turning the dial.

'Hey hey hey!' said Fiona, before being diverted by the sound of the doorbell.

The party was over. I hung back while the parents came and, one after another, the children were called away. In the middle of the confusion, the sound of his voice in the hall brought an unexpected pang, and I turned to pick up wrapping paper at the far end of the room.

'Evie!'

He had arrived in the doorway. I was starting to run out of things to clear off the floor when I sensed Evie standing beside me – a little too close, the way children do.

'Just give it back,' said Seán's voice, though this was what she was already doing; wrapping the wires around the iPod, as she held it out towards me.

'Thank you, Gina,' she said.

Gina, no less.

'You're welcome,' I said.

'Good girl.'

Seán's voice was so cold, it was clear what he really wanted to say. He wanted to say, 'Please step away from my child,' and this was very unfair. It was so unfair, that I turned and looked straight at him.

'Oh, hello,' I said.

He looked just like himself.

'Come on,' he said, ushering Evie through the doorway. The rudeness was astonishing. But he faltered and turned back for a moment, and the look he gave me then was so mute, so full of things I could not understand, that I almost forgave him.

I TRIED TO KEEP IT AT BAY, and failed. When the last small guest was gone and the rubbish bag full of packaging and uneaten lasagne the thought of him – the fact of him – happened in my chest, like a distant disaster. Something snapped or was broken. And I did not know how bad the damage was.

My hands, as they picked up the heavy jug Fiona used for juice, remembered the solid span of his waist under them that night in Montreux. What was it he had said again? 'You have lovely skin.' It seemed a bit all-purpose, at the time. 'So soft.' Why did men need to persuade themselves? Why did they have to have you, and make you up at the same time?

This, I asked myself, rather foolishly, while holding the thick glass jug in Fiona's open-plan kitchen in Enniskerry, standing on her new limestone floor (the old terracotta floor was 'all wrong' apparently). I thought about the difference between one man and another when you have your eyes closed. And I said to myself that the difference was enormous. There was no difference greater than the difference between two men when you have your eyes closed. And in my head I dropped the jug and was devastated by its fall. Fiona was loading the dishwasher. Joan was taking the plates out again and rinsing them under the tap. Megan and Jack had disappeared. I could feel it, still there under my hands: thick blown glass with swirls, in the base, of cobalt blue. Such a beautiful jug. And then I let it go.

SHE HAD FITS, apparently. This is what Fiona told me when she had cleared the last shards of glass, not just with a brush but also with the Hoover, because she didn't care about the jug so much as the danger to her children's bare feet. Evie, she said, had fits. Fiona had never actually seen it happen, though for a few years they were all on red alert. The child's mother was driven frantic; had tried everything, from consultants to – whatever – homeopathic magnets.

'She looked all right to me,' I said.

'No, she's fine now,' said Fiona. 'I think she's fine.'

'She's a funny little person,' I said.

'Is she? I don't know. I mean, everyone was so worried about her. But I don't know.'

'God. Poor Seán,' I said.

She gave me a look, exaggeratedly blank.

'Up to a point,' she said.

I wanted to know what she meant by that, but she had already turned away.

I WATCHED MEGAN LATER, sprawled on the sofa, so healthy and large. Our mother was freshening up. Jack was stuck into his Nintendo. I was waiting to leave. We were all waiting, perhaps, for Shay to come home. The evening had come adrift.

'So birthday girl,' said Fiona, sitting down and hugging her daughter to her. 'How does it feel to be nine?'

'Good,' said Megan.

We sat and pretended to watch the telly. Our mother spends such a long time in the bathroom, it used to make us anxious; wondering what she was up to in there, and when she would emerge. Meanwhile, Megan brushed her own mother's hair back from her face, admired an earring, gave it a tug.

'Careful.'

And the wrangle began: Megan stretching her mother's lips into a painful smile, pulling her eyelids back into slits, while Fiona just looked at her and refused to be annoyed. They had always been like this, locked in something that wasn't exactly love, and not quite war.

'Leave your mother alone, Megan,' I said. 'You're nine, now.'

And Fiona said, 'Hah!'

'Only another twenty years to go,' said Joan. She was standing behind us in her summer trench coat and silk scarf, her mirror work done – everything the same as before, except that tiny, crucial bit better. The usual miracle.

She looked at me.

'Will we go?'

I MAY BE GETTING THINGS in the wrong order here.

I was not yet in love with Seán. Though, at any of those moments, I might have fallen in love with him. Any of them. The first moment in the garden, by the fence that wasn't there. The time he sat in the fold-up chair on the caravan site in Brittas Bay, or went to sit, and everything slowed to a standstill except us two. I could have fallen in love with him in a hotel corridor in Switzerland, when the lock whirred and he stayed to kiss me instead of obliging me through the door.

But I did not love him. I was slightly repulsed by him, in fact. I mean I had already slept with this man, what else was there to be done with him?

If you asked me now, of course, I would say I was crazy about him from that first glance, I was in love with his hands as I watched them move in Montreux, I was in love with some other thing from the time he ushered Evie away from me and turned back in the hall – his particular sadness, whatever it might be. So don't ask me when this happened, or that happened. Before or after seems beside the point. As far as I am concerned they were happening all along.

And there are things I have forgotten to mention – the beauty of the children on the beach in Brittas that day seems important now, in a way I did not realise then. Perhaps it is the fact that Evie was not well, and I did not know it, but the beauty of the children matters in some way I do not understand.

Still, I can't be too bothered here, with chronology. The idea that if you tell it, one thing after another, then everything will make sense.

It doesn't make sense.

My mother had that old-fashioned thing, an easy death. But not yet.

And I was in love with Seán, but not as far as I knew. Not yet.

I was leaving my husband, though I might have already

left him. We might have never been together – all those times, when we thought we were. When he turned and smiled at me, at the top of the aisle in Terenure church. When he dived below me, so deep you could see the water between us thickening to green.

There are dates I can be sure of, certainly, but they are not the important ones. I can't remember the day – the hour – when Joan's 'poor form' became 'depression', for example, or when the depression turned into something physical and harder to name. There must have been a moment, or an accumulation of moments, when we stopped listening to the words she said, and started listening to the way she said them. There must have been a day when we stopped listening to her at all – one single split second, when she changed from being our mother, *Oh Joan, would you ever* . . . and turned into the harmless object of our concern.

'How are you, darling? All right?'

I was busy of course – I mean, we were all busy – but if I had recognised that moment then things might have been different. If I had been able to see her, instead of being surrounded by her, my beautiful mother, then she might still be alive.

There are some things I am sure of.

What happened, I mean the verifiable truth, reconstructible through emails here on my computer, calendar entries, phone calls made and received, was that, yes, undoubtedly, a few weeks after Megan's party, I recommended Seán, and Seán's consultancy, when we wanted to restructure in Dublin before setting up in Poland. I did it without hesitation; he was, undoubtedly the best person for the job.

All that is certain.

Slightly less certain is the fact that Conor and I had, for a while, perhaps around this time, excessive and unfriendly sex, in our sanctioned – blessed even – marriage bed.

But when it comes to Conor, I really can't go into it. I mean I can't even be bothered to remember what happened when; I am not going to map our decline. There is nothing more sordid, if you ask me, than the details.

Was the sex bad then, or was it just bad after I had started sleeping with Seán?

Bad is not the word for it.

The sex was, around this time, a little too interesting, even for me. But it was also beside the point – and maybe this is the interesting thing, that, in a story that is supposed to be about sleeping with one man or another, our bodies did not always play the game in the expected way.

But it is probably true that, around this time, we were actively thinking, or pretending to think, about starting a baby. One night, after a friend's wedding in Galway and much dancing, when I had forgotten to pack the pill and Conor said, 'What the hell.'

I can't remember what it was like exactly, but I do remember that I did not like it. Apart from anything else, the sex was terrible, it was not like sex at all.

'He's fucking my life,' I kept thinking. 'He's fucking my entire life.'

IN THESE SHOES?

RATHLIN COMMUNICATIONS PUTS European companies on the English-language web. That's what we do. But we make it look like fun.

Our office is all stripped brickwork with industrial skylights, and there is a discreet feel to the way the space is managed, an illusion of privacy which, as anyone who works in open-plan will know, just makes it worse – the paranoia, I mean. The best thing about the place is the plants contract, which is held by the boss's otherwise challenged daughter. She comes in each morning to do the foliage, which is everywhere and fabulous, from the bougainvillaea going up the ironwork to the ivy cladding the bathroom walls. The Danes who did the refurbishment put in irrigation the way you might do the wiring so the place is a thicket, and though I am cynical about these things (the idea that a few plants make us more 'green') I even voted for canaries, at some meeting, only to be outvoted on the grounds of canary shit.

It is the kind of place where the lift is big enough to bring your bike upstairs, and the coffee is all fair trade. There is an amount of sex in the air, I suppose, but we're not that pushed. We're all pretty young. We are big on ideas: the guys who have a bed in their office are sad techie bastards who really do fold them out for a sleep.

He was sitting in the meeting room, that first morning. I saw him through the glass wall before he saw me and I couldn't think what was wrong with him. He was using a fountain pen – but that was all right, wasn't it? – his BlackBerry was neatly displayed on the table beside him. The suit was maybe a bit sharp, his tie a bit restrained – but I mean, he's a consultant, he is supposed to wear a suit. Maybe it was his hair, which seemed straighter than before, and flopped forward. Had he dyed it? There was, at least, an amount of gel involved. He looked up from under this youthful mop as I walked in and he said, 'Hello, you.'

'Hi.'

He had a pair of Ray-Bans hooked on to the idle forefinger of his left hand.

'You got here,' I said.

He let the glasses swing.

'So it would appear.'

He seemed so sure we would sleep together that I decided against it on the spot, or wished, at least, for darkness to take it away, this unexpected weakness he had for props.

I sat down, smiled neatly, and said, 'So, how would you like to be introduced?'

The room filled and the meeting went ahead and it was all very much as you might expect. There was the usual blather from Frank, who was being edged out to blather elsewhere.

This was followed by a little posturing from my young colleagues, David and Fiachra, who were maddened by the potential gap. The boss was excited; you could tell he was excited because he seemed so bored. And I – well, I, as ever, smiled, facilitated, and kept clear, because I was the girl who would win in the end, despite the fact that girls so rarely do.

Seán looked from one speaker to the next, asked some questions, and kept his opinions to himself. This surprised me a little. I had expected more of the flamboyance we saw at the whiteboard in Montreux, but Seán at work – I have always loved Seán at work – used no more energy than was needful. It reminded me a little of Evie, this ability he had to be simple, in the middle of much fuss. So I managed to forget the hair gel and the horrible architect's watch, and I just looked at him thinking, for a while; his grey eyes moving from one person to the next. And – it might have been a work thing, this sensible, almost offhand way we had of speaking about, let's face it, a lot of money; it might have been the fact that he was sitting in the place where I spend most of my waking hours; but it was very intimate and slightly dreamlike to see him there – like having a movie star in your kitchen, drinking tea – and I really wanted to fuck him, then. There was, for the first time, no other word for it. I wanted to make him real. A man I would cross the street to avoid at nine o'clock – by nine twenty-five I wanted to fuck him until he wept. My legs trembled with it. My voice floated out of my mouth when I opened it to speak. The glass wall of the meeting room was huge and suddenly too transparent, I felt so exposed.

Not that things always go the way you might expect. Six

months later Frank – who still does nothing but blather – was, for reasons I can't quite fathom, running much of the show; it was David who had been edged out, to do his posturing elsewhere. Fiachra, meanwhile, had got himself a new baby, an ecstatic look in his eye and a tendency to fall asleep while sitting on the toilet, much to the delight of the entire company who tiptoed in, girls included, to listen to the sound of his snoring on the other side of the cubicle door. I was still cheerful and useful and altogether indispensable, and still going nowhere in Rathlin Communications, despite the fact I had slept with the management consultant – something neither of us found particularly relevant: I mean, no one would ever accuse Seán of securing the contract with his dick. Six months later, I was talking to the bank about going out on my own and the bank was licking me slowly all over – as were, now that I pause to think of it, both Seán Vallely and Conor Shiels. I am not an extraordinary woman but this was my life that year, and yes, it felt astonishing. It also felt like a mess. The opposite of a nervous breakdown, whatever you might call that.

But I am getting ahead of myself here.

The office game was another game for us to play, after the suburban couples game, and before the game of hotel assignations and fabulous, illicit lust, and neither of us thought there might come a moment when all the games would stop.

It was a lot of fun.

They say consultants always recommend that you lose thirty per cent – that this is what they are actually hired to say – so when Seán was finished his report, we might be moved up, or out. People found it exciting when he walked out of the lift. You knew he was there. I followed his presence through the glades of rubber plant and bamboo, listened to the click of his briefcase opening two desks down and waited for his soft voice on the phone. He might have just put his head around my partition of fern, but his courtship was close and elaborate. Every time we spoke, it was as though we were rehearsing the lie.

'Is that you?' he might say, when I picked up.

'Yes.'

I had never had an affair before. I did not realise how sexy it was to be clandestine. The secret was everything.

'Are you at your desk?'

'What do you think?'

I could hear him move and murmur a few metres away, but his real words were close, almost warm in my ear.

'Busy?'

'I am now . . .'

'What are you doing?

'Well, I'm talking to you.'

The intimacy between us was so formal, so completely erotic.

'I thought we might do that better over lunch.'

'Lovely.'

Mind you, there was a certain key-jangling element to it, too; the idea that he might be reaching rather ardently into his pocket to check for spare change. The whole thing played surprisingly close to farce. I'm not sure how many people around us knew what was going on – at a guess, they all did, and they were all hugely amused by it. But we were pretty amused too – I mean, the rutting aside, the fierce and fleeting idea of it that ran across our minds (I must confess) from time to time – we also found it slightly hilarious; the thought that we might, for once, just *get away with it*. And this is how we overcame our doubts – because we both had major doubts. When it came to the point, some weeks later, of taking each other's clothes off, we didn't weep, or declare undying love, we didn't savage each other up against some filing cabinet, we just laughed – well why not? We laughed when we kissed and we laughed at every button and reluctant zip, and it was all hunger and recognition and delight.

Meanwhile, I saw him at the coffee maker and the beauty of his tie did not offend me. I even got to like his fountain pen. I was with him all the time. He knew I was there – I was getting inside his skin. The tap of his hand on the side of his thigh. The way he leaned back in the chair and rubbed his nipple, for comfort or reward; he saw me noticing this, and stopped.

Oh, the game. The game.

The little surges of irritation, of contempt: from him, from me. *Is this what you want?*

If Seán were less of a tactical person, the thing might have gone sour before we'd even begun, but he knew his pleasures – more than I did, it has to be said. He knew when to put the phone down. When to go home. When to turn away.

It is no wonder I became obsessed.

We had lunch every Friday for five weeks; it was our debrief. We went to La Stampa – fancy but not too fancy – and talked business. He was good, as I keep saying, at his job. He had no interest in complication. He looked at the company carefully, trying to split the rock with just one tap. And after business, came charm. He told a story, he told another. Really funny stories. He ordered dessert wine. He teased me about the 'posh' school I went to, about the height of my heels, he made me fight and flirt. I thought, by week three, that there was something wrong with my blood pressure, that I might actually faint or die.

I took to walking home in the evening – or walking somewhere. I swerved from the entrance of the pub on a Friday, because he was not there. I veered from the pedestrian light that was against me, crossed streets because they were empty of traffic, and turned different corners – not so much avoiding home as averse to any particular destination. One night, I ended up on the rim of Dublin Bay. It was October by then; dark and cold. There was a container ship lodged on the horizon, impossibly large and disproportionate. The endless strand gave way in the darkness to a sea so shallow you would think the thing was stuck to the sea floor. But the lights floated in front of me. The ship was moving, or it must have been moving. I could not tell, in the darkness, which way.

It was also beautiful, this game of not touching: that is the thing I am afraid to say about myself and Seán – how beautiful it was, how exquisite the distance we kept between us. And when I saw him one afternoon standing by the printer, lost in thought, with the light falling over his shoulders, it was as though the same light had jabbed me in the chest. I hadn't expected to find him there. He was wearing grey and his hair was grey: the plants beside him were dark green and the floor of the corridor beyond was teal blue. These are the details and they sound so foolish: a middle-aged man in an office with a file in his hand – I mean to say. And there was no solace in his absence, either. When he was gone, I thought about nothing else: Seán in my sister's garden, Seán in Brittas, Seán in Switzerland. I wondered where he was this minute, and what he might be doing. I thought about a future together and wiped the thought, fifty, sixty, a hundred times a day. It was all such an agitation. But somewhere in the gaps – in the certainty of seeing him after the lift doors opened, or in the shock of his voice nearby – a stillness hit, a kind of perfection. It was very beautiful, this desire that opened inside me, and then opened again. And this is what puts me beyond regret: the sweetness of my want for Seán Vallely, the sense of something unutterable at the heart of it. I felt – I still feel – that if we kissed again, we might never stop.

I lost half a stone.

Which was brilliant. I bounced into work and I ran up the stairs, too impatient for the lift. And I very seldom placed my forehead against a convenient wall, and pushed.

It is surprising how close you can get to someone, by staying very still.

There are two things I noticed, and I don't know if they are different or connected. First of all, in the office, there was this thing he did if I knew something he didn't, or if I had been somewhere he had yet to go – that scuba-diving holiday in Australia, for example, or my ease with languages, which was in such contrast to his own few bits of French – he managed very quickly to be proud of these achievements, to boast about them on my behalf. And this irritated me: he made it sound like he was responsible for my being so generally clever and gung ho. So it was as if I did the Great Barrier Reef and he got the credit. Or at the very least that we were in the whole Reef business together. And of course we were. I mean, who doesn't like Australia? By the time he had finished, the whole damn continent seemed to belong to him. And all this because he had never actually been there, and I had.

You had to admire it, as a way of turning all things to the good.

'Been there, done that,' he might say. 'Isn't she great?'

But it didn't make me feel great. I wanted to be free of it, this bag he kept putting me in. It got so I wanted to sleep with him – to love him even – just to be myself again, undescribed. But most of all, I wanted him not to be jealous of me in the first place. I mean, it was only a question of getting on a plane. This was before I heard about his childhood, of course, and long before I realised that he didn't want this particular emotion fixed. He liked being jealous, it was his comfort and company – call it ambition; it was his protection from the night.

The other thing I noticed was that Seán doesn't really like eating. I don't mean he doesn't like food, I mean he hates all the chewing and swallowing – I suppose there is much to dislike. Despite which, there was always huge restaurant palaver: the choice of table, the crack of the napkin, endless discussion about the wine, and a vague prissiness about pasta that was not home-made. The foreplay, you might say, went on forever. Then the food would arrive and he would wait. He might fold his hands together and finish his point, or make another point. Finally, he would take that ceremonial first bite, go Mmmm mmmm, and praise the dish: the toffee-ness of the cherry tomatoes, or some such. Then, a bit of ordinary eating – chomp chomp – until the moment I realised he had stopped and was looking at the food. He might attempt another forkful but lose heart before it entered his mouth. Then a bit more staring; a kind of altercation. Finally, he would stage some distraction, grab a last morsel, and push away the plate.

Then he would look up at my, still-chewing, mouth.

I was in love with this man – clearly I was in love, or at least obsessed; the rhythms of his appetite were something I took so personally. But God knows, I could eat for Ireland, so I always felt a bit lonely after our lunch dates; not just greedy, but also thwarted or rejected, as if the food was all my fault.

'Wonderful,' he would say. 'Have you ever had it with pesto?'

I wondered what it would be like to live with that across the table from you, breakfast lunch and dinner. Did they all wait with their tongues hanging out, until he gave the nod? Did they stop when he stopped? Aileen, it seemed to me, was the kind of woman who would count the number of peas she put on your plate. All that containment.

I'm afraid Evie doesn't eat ice-pops, do you, Evie?

Either they were a perfect match, I thought, or they hadn't had sex in years. Once the idea came to me, it made enormous sense. This was why they were so neat and polite. This was the sadness in the look he gave me, when he turned back in Fiona's hall.

But, though I lost seven – count 'em – pounds, living on love alone, I did not think about Aileen much in those office weeks. To be honest, I forgot that Aileen, or even Conor, might exist. When I came home, I was sometimes surprised to find him in the house. He seemed so large and so real.

Who are you?

Such is the delight of a long working day.

We made love properly for the first time, myself and Seán, early one evening, after we rolled back from our Friday lunch and rolled into a party for a guy who was taking a year out to be with his yacht. We managed to linger after everyone had gone, and the details of what corner we found and what we did; how we managed it, and who put what where, are nobody's business but our own.

SECRET LOVE

WHAT IS IT ABOUT WIVES? There is this thing they do – because I am not the only one this has happened to. I am not the only one who was invited in.

I picked up the phone one day before Christmas and I heard the person on the other end of the line say:

'Oh hello, I am looking for Gina Moynihan.'

'That's me!'

'Hi Gina, this is Aileen – you know, Seán Vallely's wife?'

And I thought, *She has found us out.*

I remember every word of the conversation that followed; every bare syllable and polite inflection. I played it in my head for days afterwards, note perfect. I could sing it, like a song.

'Oh, hi,' I said. A little too fast. With a slight choke on the 'Oh'. It might, if you were listening very closely, have sounded more like, 'Go hi'. Aileen, however, did not miss a beat.

'I got your number from Fiona, I hope you don't mind. I wanted to invite you over, after Christmas. We have our New Year's Day brunch, I don't know if Fiona ever mentioned it, we just do a sort of brunch, and Seán does that consommé thing with vodka, for people who need a cure. What do you call them?'

It was the most words I had heard out of her in one go. It took me a second to realise she had stopped.

'Bull Shots?' My voice sounded strange. As well it might.

'That's the one. It's from eleven thirty, though people wander in any time.'

She wasn't giving me a chance to refuse, or indeed to accept. She said, 'Seán would love to see you, and Donal of course.'

Donal?

'Lovely,' I said.

Maybe she meant Conor.

'You know where we are – the one on the corner as you take the left up to Fiona's.'

'Yes, I think so,' I said.

'The rough grey wall?'

'Rough' that was nice. She did not say, 'the old granite wall', she was much too tactful for that.

Nor did she mention – why should she? – the night I had parked opposite that wall and looked up at her house for two hours, until, one by one, the lights went out. I don't know why I did this. Fiona and Shay were in Mount Juliet for the weekend, so there was no risk of them passing by and recognising the car: that was certainly a factor. I wanted to be close to him, I suppose. I wanted to see the cube of light in which he sat. I also wanted to discover if they still slept, Aileen and Seán, in the same room. I let the car window down. The night air was completely still. Front window bright: front window dark. A baffled light from the back of the house, blocked by corners and half-open doors. Off. A different light turned on. A head rising and dipping, in silhouette, on what must be the landing – that middle window above the door. They have a house like a child's drawing of a house; sweet and square.

No one puts the cat out.

By 1 a.m. I am no further on.

I am cold though, and so drained by the excitement of that head bobbing on the landing that I can hardly prise my fingers off the steering wheel to start the damn car.

But of course Aileen did not mention this on the phone. She didn't say, 'If you like the house so much you might as well knock at the door.' She just said, very tactfully, 'The rough grey wall,' and I said, 'Aha.'

I have a fluffy ended biro on my desk; a gift from my niece when she was five or six. It pokes out of my pen holder; a ballerina in a froth of blue feathers, and I stroke my face with her when I am on the phone sometimes, while the feathers twitch and waft about in the breeze of my breath. Or I look at her face, which is always smiling.

'I think I know it,' I said. 'New Year's Day?'

'You will come. Brilliant,' said Aileen. 'I hope so anyway. Bye!'

'Bye,' I said, but she was already gone.

Aileen as socialite, ticking the calls off her list. She did not give me a chance to turn her down. Clever Aileen, no pressure, just a bit of fun. Competent Aileen. Aileen whose little fat sits in sad, middle-aged pouches about her boy's body, who is too busy, God knows, to bother about such things, and what is there to be done, anyway, when you're on the damn Cross-trainer three times a week. Busy with the house and with the garden. Busy with the shopping. And the cleaning. Busy with the child. Does she have a job? I think so, though I never asked, and it is certainly too late now, to pause while teasing the lobe of my lover's ear to whisper, 'So what does your wife do all day?' into its red concavities.

She doesn't know, I decide. If she knew, or even suspected, she would get Conor's name right.

Or maybe she does know, and got it wrong for fun.

We had met, by the time of his wife's weird social impulse, two more times. There was no doubt the first time, no hesitation. We agreed, smiling, to a Northside lunch and, as I made my way up O'Connell Street, I got a text from his phone that read:

'The Gresham 328.'

That was all. No, 'I need to see you,' no, 'I will wait for you there.'

There was nothing before the second assignation either; ten long days later in a hotel out by the airport. No rude talk, no photo enclosed of something untoward.

Just: 'Clarion 29'.

And from me: 'OK'.

We discussed, on each occasion, the decor; the pictures on the walls and the colour of the carpet: a hearty, natural brown in the Gresham and a strangely non-existent green in the airport hotel, where all the guests were on their way through. Seán had booked and paid each time – at a guess in cash. It was like we were born to it. No emails, no paper trail, just two, instantly deleted texts.

And inside this scaffolding we had erected of jaunty, fake arrangements and silence, after the bare number on my phone's display, and the walk past reception where no one bothers to call my name, when the door has been found and knocked upon, the thoughtful champagne uncorked and, eyes averted, with a terrible small smile on both our lips, the carpet discussed, we had – I don't know if 'sex' is the word for it, although it was also, quite definitely, sex – we did, or had, just what we wanted, and when that wasn't enough, we pushed it farther, and had some more.

We didn't talk much.

Silence made it that bit filthier, of course. And people do not speak, in a dream. Or if they speak, it is not in a real way. I think about how quiet it was in those two rooms as we made our way through the deliberate and surprising actions that brought us skin to skin. It was daylight. You could hear the Friday afternoon traffic and, at two o'clock, the clock chimes from the GPO. There wasn't much kissing. Maybe this is why it all seemed so clear – too clear – why so few words were said.

But also, perhaps, because there was too much to say, and all of it wrong.

Or maybe I am being romantic, here. I mean, who knows what Seán was thinking, at that stage. He did say – I think I remember him saying – 'Sssh.'

And, actually, that first time in the Gresham was a bit hurried and mishandled. Seán afterwards a little agitated, almost brusque. But the second time. The second assignation. Was perfect.

What was he like in bed? He was like himself. Seán is the same in bed as he is the rest of the time. The connection is easy to see, when you have made it once, but before you do, it is one of the great mysteries: *What is he like?*

This.

And this.

I watched him dress, in the airport hotel, and I stayed on after he left for his flight. I said I wanted a shower, but I did not take a shower. I got up and sat on the chair and looked at our after-image, his towel abandoned on the floor, the final print, on the wrinkled sheets, of the movements we had made. Then I pulled on my clothes and went out to the bar, where I sat in the secret hum of his scent and drank one single whiskey and watched, all about me, a mayhem of dragged suitcases and flights diverted and sad farewells.

'We drove up from Donegal, the day,' a woman said to me, with tears in her eyes, and a pint of lager in front of her. 'She's off in the morning,' indicating a woman of great age and girth on the banquette beside her, with hair done up, like my country grandmother's, in a thin, grey wrapover braid.

The old woman, whose clothes and teeth were all American, nodded to me mournfully, while across the bar, three big slabs of young-fellas checked me out, then turned their attention to the big-screen TV.

The bedroom, when I walked back to it, was truly empty. Even our ghosts were gone. Or perhaps there was something left – I tried to leave the door open but glanced back at the last moment and pulled it shut behind me instead.

I handed the key in at reception: four space-age consoles on stalks, each manned by an Eastern European with a crisp manner in a black suit. I chose the shortest queue and a blonde receptionist, with 'Sveva' on her name tag. I had plenty of time to read it – whatever the problem with the couple ahead of me was, by the time I got to her, we were old friends. She checked her console screen and said, 'Yes, that's all been taken care of,' and gave me a smile, bright with indifference, and I thought – I wanted to ask her, suddenly – *Where will it end?*

THREE DAYS LATER, with her wonderful sense of timing, Aileen rang, like a woman arriving in a panic as the ship pulls away from the quay. She was too late. We had already embarked – isn't that the word that people use? – on our affair.

Back in the office, the flirtation had died. I loved the blank look I gave him beside the coffee machine, the indifferent, 'See you tomorrow,' as I pulled my coat off its hook. This was the power our secret gave us. As far as the gossip was concerned, the trail had gone cold.

This must be the rule; that people are madly obvious before they get it together and pathetically obvious when it all stops – but when it is all happening, when the deal is done and they're at it like knives, then they are as quiet as a government minister with an account in the Cayman Islands, and twice as good at helping old ladies across the street.

'Hi Seán, sorry about the Poles. I'm still after them to get the numbers for you. They say Thursday. Is that all right?'

'It'll have to do.'

'I'll keep pushing,' I say, desire like a kick of blood, that hits low down, then spreads all through me, delicious and alight. It is contained, held by the secret, my skin is the exact shape of it, because I am the secret, *I am the money*, and this makes me feel I could do anything.

Anything.

Except tell anyone, of course. Which means I can do nothing, in actual fact, in real life. Except be still and know.

'Thursday,' you say. 'What's that in Polish?'

'Czwartek.'

'Oooh. Nice.'

BUT THE DEAL WAS NOT DONE after the first meeting in the Gresham Hotel. Nothing was certain, afterwards. If anything, he seemed disappointed – with himself, with me, with the inevitability of it all.

'Give it five minutes,' he said, when I tried to leave with him.

He placed his finger against my lips, rough and human, and then he was gone, leaving me to the blank walls and the digital display of the hotel clock, which refused to change. Five minutes. I stood by the window and saw him emerge on to the street below, bareheaded, hunched under the November drizzle.

That was it.

No arrangements, no hint of an arrangement.

Which might explain my little lapse outside his gate a week later, sitting in my car until after midnight, hanging on to the steering wheel. Because a week waiting for him to call is a very long time. You could go mad in a week.

You could go mad in an afternoon.

Our hands met, once. In bed. I remembered the shock.

Our hands touched when we were otherwise naked and busy, and it was actually embarrassing – such was the charge of reality they held. I apologised, the way you might to a stranger you brush against in the street.

For a week, after the Gresham Hotel, I pulled his love towards me, sitting utterly still and thinking of nothing but the next split second, and then the next, when he would materialise, smiling, in front of me, or my phone would jump at his call.

But it did not jump. No matter how many split seconds I imagined, in how many long days, it just refused.

I did meet him sometimes, of course: I passed his desk, he passed mine. We discussed, on one occasion, the hidden calories in your average café latte. And then he moved on.

At home, I was cross with Conor all the time. How could he be with me all evening, eat Indian takeaway, watch 'The Sopranos', and not realise the turmoil I was in? If love was a kind of knowledge then he could not love me, because he hadn't the faintest clue. It was a strange feeling. Some fundamental force had been removed from our love; like telling the world there was no such thing as gravity, after all. He did not know me. He did not know his own bed.

I turned from him at night or, maybe just once, suffered his attentions – for the misery of it, and the solace. I got up at 4 a.m., to eat cereal straight from the box, with spoonfuls of peanut butter on the side. I woke in the early morning and dressed and redressed; high heels, higher. Then I climbed down off the heels and put on my flats, and buttoned my blouse back up, and went to work. And, on Sunday night, eight days after

I left that room in the Gresham Hotel, I found myself outside Seán's gate in the darkness, hanging on to the steering wheel, making deals, casting spells.

On Monday, I bought him something.

The local vegetable shop is a little yuppie shed, open to the elements. In December it has boxes of Christmas satsumas, green figs, pomegranates woven about by white mesh in figures of eight. I chose a little bag of lychees, cold and bumpy to the touch. I ate one on the way back to the office, standing in a doorway and sheltering from the rain. I had never tasted them fresh, before. The skin was like bark; so thick you could hear it tear. Under it was the dark white of the fruit; smooth as a boiled egg and more slippy, and in the middle of this grey, scented flesh was a deep red pip, surrounded by its own pink stain.

We had been talking about China. Seán had said I should learn some Mandarin. He said he was in Shanghai – had I ever been to Shanghai? It was like the fucking wild west out there – and he nearly bought a Teach Yourself DVD for his daughter in the airport, though she was past that stage where they sort of sing their way into speech, that perfect stage, when you understand how Chinese got invented in the first place. He said you got on those roads, those eight-lane highways, completely empty, and you understood something about the future – that you could do it. Certainly, it was scary. But the future was also *normal*.

But no, I had never been to Shanghai. I put the little bag, still spotted with rain, on his desk. Is this what I wanted to say? – what is under the skin, stays under the skin. That I was willing to keep things small.

'Where would you book,' he said to me later, 'if you needed an airport hotel?'

'The Clarion?' I said.

And three days after I shut the door of that second hotel room behind me, and caught a minibus up to the airport terminal, and got in the taxi queue, and went home unwashed and beyond caring, I answered the phone and found myself talking to his wife, being invited by his wife; who wanted, presumably, a good look at me, now that it was all too late.

It made me more sad, than anything. I put down the phone, and waved my little feather ballerina about, in an admonishing way.

Now see what you have done.

KISS ME, HONEY, HONEY, KISS ME

MEANWHILE, THERE WAS THE OFFICE PARTY to get through. At 9 p.m., I am standing in the hallway of l'Gueuleton in Fade Street, saying goodbye to Fiachra who is trying to get out the door and go home to his pregnant wife. When he succeeds, Seán, who was assisting, finds the wall with his back and tips his head against the brickwork – once, twice – saying, 'Fuck. Fuck.' I say, 'Where can we go?' and he says, 'We can't go, we just can't,' but we are both quite drunk and end up dragging each other into the Drury Street car park for another endless kiss in some concrete corner that smells of petrol and the rain, with the sound of people wandering through the far levels and the squawk of found cars answering the remote.

And this, too, is another epic kiss, a wall-slider if there ever was one, I feel like I am clambering out of my own head, that the whole usual mess of myself has been put on the run by it. By the end, we are barely touching and everything is so clear and tender I find myself able to say:

'When will I see you?' and he says, 'I don't know. I'll try. I don't know.'

I walk through the Christmas city lights, not a taxi in sight and the town going crazy all around me, and I think how kissing is such an extravagance of nature. Like birdsong; heartfelt and lovely beyond any possible usefulness.

And then home: the bite of the key in the cold lock, the smell of the still air in the hallway, and the glow, upstairs, of Conor's laptop. I go up there – drunk, surprised each time my foot meets a step. My husband is sitting in the armchair, his face blue in the light of the screen, and nothing moves except the sweep and play of his finger on the mouse-pad and his thumb as it clicks.

'Have a good night?'

I HAD, OF COURSE, no intention of going to Aileen's damn party. But it was a long Christmas in Youghal, pulling crackers, making small-talk, tippling through each day into a state of hard sobriety that kept you awake at night, angry as a stone. Conor's family never drank in his father's pub, though sometimes one or other of them would shrug his jacket on and jump in a minicab to take a turn behind the bar. They lived out the Cork road, with a stream in the garden, and they kept themselves separate from the ordinary drunks of the town with cases of French wine, which they got from their importer in Mullingar.

Conor's mother wore cream trousers to match her ash-blonde hair, and fine gold jewellery on a permanent, light tan. His father was a big, physical man who liked to get a decent handful when he said hello; who thought a handful of daughter-in-law was, at his age, only fair. His wife might rebuke him, she might rap out a 'Thank you, Francis!' and everyone would laugh – I am not imagining this – at my discomfort, and the wonderful, horny badness of their old man.

They were a good couple, for all that. They had fun. The place was always busy with cousins and friends and various 'associates' who dropped in clutching bottles of Heidsieck or Rémy Martin and laughing about 'coals to Newcastle' as they were invited into the front room. It reminded me of my own father, the mock seriousness, 'Oh take no notice of that fella!', with its under-swell of self-importance and things unsaid; the way they were all *in the know*.

I am not sure what there was to know – my father either – I am not sure what they actually got, for all their air of being canny: the pub licence, maybe; planning permission for some bungalow. It hardly seemed worth all the nods and winks, and though it made me nostalgic for the men who tickled the back of my neck to produce fifty-pence pieces in the hall, Conor hated it – it made him literally itch in his clothes and try to shrug free.

What Conor liked about being home was the chance it gave him to be a boy again. He liked wrestling with his brothers and being a slob and leaving the kitchen work to the women, and it never ceased to astonish me. If this was regression then he was going back to some smaller self, one long ago discarded. So my rage at the sink was only partly to do with the drudgery of being a guest in that house, it was more to do with the loss of the man I knew to this loutish teenager who was a stranger, possibly, even to himself.

In bed, at night, I tried to claim him back – I was sleeping with Seán at the time, I know that, but these things don't always work the way you think they should – and some night, before the drinking got too humourless and steady, I knocked on his shaved brown head to see if he was still in there. And he was. He opened his eyes in the darkness. Then he loved me up, down and crossways, as though I was a dream of his future come impossibly true, there among his old football posters and scattered CDs, as though the truth was better than he ever could have imagined.

We did not fight until New Year's Eve. I can't remember what triggered it. Money probably. We used to fight about money. His mother. I mean, tick the list. The way the washing machine was left to flood after he 'installed' it and pushed the button and went back to play Shattered Galaxy. The whole internet thing maddened me, by then – I can't remember when it happened, when Conor at the cutting edge turned into Conor hanging out with a load of wasters online. I went so far as to check his browsing history once, but it was completely unremarkable – which just made it worse, somehow: at that stage I would have been happy to find porn.

But this could not have been the fight we had in Youghal because we were outside, far away, for once, from any screen. We were walking on the beach and the pain of the cold air on my lungs was like the pain of the view on my eyeballs, after four days of kitchen living and bad Christmas TV. It was being in the open that let it loose, I think. Even when I shouted, my voice seemed to happen in its distant echo, out where the sky grew low over the sea.

The beach was not completely empty – there was a woman walking down near the water and a man taking photographs, with a very ordinary camera, from the giant concrete steps that held the land safe from the waves. Lines of black posts marched down to the shoreline, small and smaller, overtaken, each in their turn, by the shifting sand. The new summer houses, a little toy village, tucked themselves under a distant headland. Conor said his father owned four of them, *Did you ever see the like?* But they weren't too bad. They looked almost pretty under the blue winter sky, through air so still you thought it might crack. Even the waves – or is this just the way I remember it? – even the waves made no noise.

The fight was not, in fact, about money; nor was it about the internet, or the flooded kitchen, it wasn't about the box – I remember saying this – of our lives, the colour of the box, or the smell of it, whether things worked in the box or not, but just the fact that we were in a damn box, when we might be free.

It was the last day of the year. I had decided to give up cigarettes in the morning. Maybe that was what it was all about: the yelp of the addict before it is all taken away. Or maybe it was because I was giving up for Seán, who found the smell of stale cigarettes so disgusting. So he too was looming as the day ticked on – this need I had to be right for Seán. And the anger that came with this was terrible; the pure annoyance of smashing my way out of one box, only to find myself in another one.

There is nothing like a bit of drama on an empty coastline, the shrill little screams and foot stampings entertainment for the gulls, tinnitus for the fishes. There is nothing so pointless and refreshing: a sad backside hitting a million affronted grains of sand, the faint ticking, in the rocks, of footsteps walking away.

Conor went back to the car and left me to it, to the skyline and the line where the sea lapped the shore, and I watched as the water sank into, or pulled away from the sand.

I was quite happy, then. I lit a cigarette and was happy for the length of it. Nothing moved, except the water, which was always moving. I thought the world might have stopped, except for the progress of ash down the cigarette's white shaft.

It was New Year's Eve – my least favourite day of any year – and I just didn't think I could do it, this time. I thought midnight would kill me, every strike of the damn clock. I wanted to sit where I was, and let time pass elsewhere. How do you do that? You could rise up and let the earth roll beneath you. You could float on that still, cold sea. You could love one man and never stop kissing another.

Never stop.

When I climbed back into the car, I said to Conor I was going home, that I really wanted to see my mother tonight, and he could come too if he liked but I would prefer he didn't.

'No, really prefer,' I said.

And that I just . . . wanted . . . some time . . . all right?

Conor, out of pity for this and for all sad human cliché, sighed and leaned forward to the ignition.

'I'll drive you up,' he said.

'No.'

'Well you take the car then,' he said. 'I'll catch a lift.'

And I didn't say 'Thanks,' or 'Sorry,' or 'It's not you, it's the damn cigarettes.' I neither lied to him nor told the truth – that all this had nothing to do with him, nor even, in a way, with Seán Vallely.

I HEADED FOR WATERFORD along the N25, slipping down the high curving road into Dungarvan just as the streetlights came on. I thought about my mother-in-law's face as I said my unexpected, hurried goodbye.

'Don't worry,' I might have said. 'I will not break your son's heart.'

Or something of that nature. Even if it was a lie. Even if we were to speak, which we did not, of course. The power had shifted between Conor's women, that was all, though I did not enjoy it as much as you might expect.

Conor brought the car around to the front door and I put my case in the boot. I kissed them all goodbye outside their big white bungalow, and my wretched father-in-law kept his hands to himself, for once. But you know, I never really minded flirting with my father-in-law. I probably liked it as much as anything. I am a terrible flirt.

I passed the turn off to Brittas and the one for Enniskerry at the beginning of the motorway lights. I drifted all the way to the Tallaght exit, worked my way through the suburban streets and pulled up the handbrake outside my mother's front door. I switched off the engine and stood out of the car in the winter silence, the blood in my veins still hurtling on.

It was nice to be with my own family for once. Even though I had no family to speak of, and it was just the two of us, sitting in front of the real flames of my mother's artificial gas fire, flicking channels through the midnight bells and drinking Sea Breezes.

Joan poked the ash of her cigarette vaguely at the fireplace, even though it wasn't a real fireplace, and she loosed her stockings through the cloth of her skirt, to let them settle around her ankles, in two gossamer nests. My mother was strangely slovenly, for someone who looked so pristine. Or more than pristine; for someone who seemed to gather the available light about her. It used to embarrass me, the way she sat in the kitchen with our friends after school, getting all their chat and letting the ash topple on the tiled floor. It wasn't as though she didn't have an ashtray. I found one in the fridge once – which wasn't a surprise; the contents of the fridge were often a little arbitrary. 'What do you do all day?!' I remember shouting at her, when I got in hungry one afternoon. To which she said nothing. There was nothing for her to say.

I suppose, in the early years of her widowhood, she let things slide and we did not forgive her for it. Children want things to be ordinary. Maybe that's all they want.

Ordinary was, in any case, exactly what I got that New Year's Eve: a cheese-and-tomato sandwich, a cup of tea; my mother rattling through the bottles to see if there was anything worthwhile, shaking the carton of cranberry juice, saying, 'Good for the bladder,' the pair of us going into the sitting room to talk about – it is hard to remember what we talked about, I can't quite fix it in my mind. I remember she said, 'How are the in-laws?' and I said, 'You don't want to know.'

Diets, obviously; the fact that when you get older the weight all shifts around to the front. I think we also talked about separates versus dresses, old boyfriends and what happened to them, both hers and mine. My stubborn aversion to pastels. The usual.

Then, at five past twelve she stood up and made for bed, and I did not know what to do, or where to go. Maybe she was so used to her routine, it didn't occur to her to see me to the door.

I SNIFFED THE LAST of my drink and swallowed it down.

'Am I over the limit?' I said, and triggered much fuss. Joan, for whom public transport was a deep mystery, wouldn't hear of my trying for a taxi, 'On this night of all nights,' she said.

'Oh darling. Go on up to your own room.'

She was out in the hall by then, holding the post at the foot of the stairs and her eyes, over the drag and sough of her breathing, were large with concern.

'Well, let me help you up at least,' I said, but she batted me vaguely away, and started up by herself, holding on to the banister.

'Just tonight, mind!'

In case I thought the burden of care was about to shift my way.

I followed her up and went into my old bedroom, climbed into bed and undressed piecemeal between sheets slick with the cold. In the morning, I woke like a child and came down to a breakfast of eggs and sausage, toast, butter, tea. My mother was already dressed in a raspberry cashmere twinset and tweed skirt, her make-up done – just a few crow's feet, she really had remarkable skin. She gave out to me for my cheap tights, and sent me upstairs for a new packet of stockings from her drawer: 'Mother, I am thirty-two years old.'

I refused the stockings, but found a huge costume ring she had from her dancing days and borrowed that instead. I nearly took a scarf, too, but some sadness made me put it back at the last minute, saying, 'I don't know when I'll get it back to you.'

Then we got into her Renault and drove out to Bray where my brother-in-law was doing the New Year swim.

We made our way through the deserted town and parked along the seafront. It took us a while to find him among the crowd on the beach; my sister's pantomime husband, dressed in a fright wig and a yellow T-shirt with 'Aware' written on the front. He was collecting 'for depression' he said, while his children pushed back against Fiona's legs and gazed up at him, frozen and bemused. He looked fat. Or worse than fat, I thought – what with the belly and the legs made spindly by black lycra – he looked middle-aged. His feet, especially, were horrible; waxy and white on the stones of the beach, as he struggled his way down to the deep, churning water and the shrieking masochism of the crowd. They splashed about, and turned to wave at the shore, and it made me uneasy, seeing people swim in Halloween masks or bobbly hats, the way the guy beside you took off his coat and turned into a madman, who didn't know the difference between wet and dry.

Afterwards, we went back to Enniskerry for soup and a cup of tea, and our mother stayed to babysit, while we walked up to Seán and Aileen's for the Bull Shot cure.

So it was all natural and ordained and as it should be that, at 2 p.m., I was walking in a righteous way across the New Year's gravel to the matt grey door belonging to my colleague and acquaintance Seán Vallely, with the hand-shaped knocker on it, that his wife had brought back from Spain.

The house was not as large as I remembered it from the night I sat and watched the lights go out. Somehow, in the days after my little stalking incident, it had grown in my mind to be a square Georgian farmhouse, with an unspecified acreage in front and behind. But in fact, it was only semi-detached, and the windows – one on either side of the door, and three in a row upstairs – were not that large. Still, it had that thing. It had lollipop bay trees with red Christmas bows, it had tasteful white lights dripping from the eaves, it had that Cotswold gravel and box hedge *thing* that I hated and wanted in exactly equal measure, and I walked up to the threshold with badness on my mind.

'Nice knocker,' I said, picking up the slender brass fingers and letting them fall. Then I fixed my gaze on the painted wood, and waited for it to swing away.

And when the door opened, there was no one there.

Of course, it was Evie on the other side, and this threw me. I had to look down from the piece of air where I expected an adult face, and my expression, when I found her, may have slipped from my control. She looked at me with that curious, caught gaze of hers and Fiona said, 'You remember Megan's Auntie?'

'Yes,' though there was nothing in her voice that would make you believe it.

Then she said, 'Hi, Gina.'

And I said, 'Hello, sweetheart,' because that was exactly what she was, gathering coats in her stunned, delighted way and bringing them up the narrow stairs to be left on some unspecified bed above.

I had not thought about Evie, all this time. I don't know why. The fact of the wife was always there, she was like a wall running along the side of my mind, but when you are in the throes of lust for a man you do not – maybe you just can't – think about his daughter. As far as I was concerned, Evie was irrelevant to the whole business of sleeping with Seán, her shadow did not, could not, fall across our hotel bed. It would be wrong for her to exist at such a moment: it would be slightly obscene. Or less than obscene – it just wouldn't make sense.

And now, there she was. The fact of her amazed me. I had intimations of some dark future, as I watched her walk up the stairs with my coat laid across her two forearms. Or, worse than that: there was a word I wanted to shout at her ascending back, something blurted and bizarre, like:

'Little cow!'

But I did not know what word it was, or what kind of drama it came from. 'Assassin!' Was that Miss Brodie, or Baby Jane? When I was at school, we went to see *Hamlet* and, during Ophelia's mad scene, a girl from some inner-city school, a little barrel-chested one with unwashed hair, stood up in front of me and roared, 'Ah, show us your cunt!' at the actress onstage.

That was what it was like. A bit.

Of course I did not want to shout this, or anything like it, at the child. I had no words for the shout in my head, and no intention of looking for them, but it was, whatever way it took me, a giddy moment. Standing for the first time in the smell of Seán Vallely's domestic life – all Christmas orange and clove – watching the neat and lovely back of his daughter ascending the stairs, her arms held carefully out in front of her; her white socks, the fresh and secret skin at the backs of her knees, like a child from the fifties – I don't think you could even get Megan into a skirt by that age, unless there were leggings involved – but there she was, in a perfect little kilt and, my goodness, black patent leather shoes.

Then Aileen was in the hall, all mock bustle and precision.

'Come in, come in!' she said, kissed us one by one, 'Happy New Year!' first Fiona, then Shay and then me.

I am trying to remember the smell or texture of her skin, or lips; the sense of her proximity, but a sort of blank thing happened when she came in for the kiss. She stood back quickly. And smiled again.

'So glad you could make it. Some of the others are inside.'

Other what?

She wasn't as old as I remembered, though she sported some very middle-aged lipstick, pinkish and pearlised, on her unprepossessing, useful face. She was wearing a black Issey Miyake pleats dress edged with turquoise, and the collar stood up around her neck in a sharp frill. It made her look like some soft creature, poking out of its beautiful, hard shell.

The house – unlike her outfit – was surprisingly unpretentious. There was a study on the right of the door we had come in, and a kitchen down at the end of the hall. On the other side, they had knocked through from front to back to make one long reception room.

'Isn't this lovely?' I said to her, taking it all in.

'Oh, it's neither fish nor fowl,' she said. 'I wanted to take out the back of it, but Seán says it's time to sell up again, move back into town.'

'How's the new house?' said Fiona.

'Well that's the thing. We love it.'

'Isn't that great?' said Fiona.

She turned to me, 'We found this wonderful old place overlooking the beach at Ballymoney. Up high,' then back to Fiona, 'When will you let Megan come down? I go straight from the school pick-up, you know, let Seán follow whenever, every second or third weekend.'

I had been hoping for clues, of course, but I was surprised to get them hurled at me as soon as I walked in the door. It was not that Aileen wanted me to know about her second house – everyone over forty wants you to know about their second house – she was actually telling me her schedule. She was spelling it out for me: my husband is free every second (or third) Friday, but on Saturday he gets in the car and follows me down to the country where we light a fire, and drink a bottle of good red, and look, *from on high*, at the lovely, ever-changing sea.

And all this before I had a drink in my hand.

'Oh how nice,' I said, for distraction, looking at the series of photographs on the wall. There was a line of them in square, dark frames; the images in flaring, overexposed, black and white. It took me a moment to recognise Evie in one, then another – these were studio pictures, taken when she was a toddler. Very arty and beautiful. Aileen in a white shirt, leaning against a white wall. A tousle-headed Seán.

I thought I heard his voice from the kitchen and took a quick left into the long living room, which was comfortably full of people. Four beautiful casement windows. Food one end, drinks by the door, a Filipino circling for the refill with a bottle in either hand.

Frank was there, a little to my surprise – blathery old Frank – he gave me a slippery look across the room, as though there was something I did not know about. For a second I thought it was to do with me and Seán, but Frank doesn't do sex, he does other kinds of hidden currents and agreements; the kinds that happen between men and are not about anything you could put a finger on – it's not the cars, it's not the football, it's about who is going to win (though win what is sometimes also a question). I say this with some bitterness, because Frank was promoted over my head three months later, so now I know. A man with no discernible talent except for being *on side.*

I gave him a nod through the various bodies and gesturing hands between us and he came over to give me a clumsy kiss, before heading home.

'Next year in Warsaw,' he said.

Poor old Frank.

I heard Seán seeing him off at the front door and I went up to the drinks table, where he might look in and spot me without having to say hello. The silence when he clocked me was very slight, and very interesting. I didn't look over at him. I smiled, as though to myself, and moved away.

I recognised a few of the faces from Fiona's parties, except there were no children here and the mothers, dolled up in the middle of the day, looked catastrophic, some of them, or else surprisingly attractive and well got.

Fiachra was also there, with his pregnant wife called – I must have got this wrong – 'Dahlia'. It was strange to meet her in the flesh – indeed in all that extra flesh; she was huge. She waved a large glass of wine at me and said, 'Do you think this will bring it on?' Then she took a sip and winced. There was a woman, she told me, who went on the lash at the Galway Film Fleadh and woke up the next morning in hospital, with the world's worst hangover and a baby in the cot beside her.

'Like, what happened last night? Where am I?'

'Respect,' I said.

'Drunk. Can you imagine? The midwives must have loved her.'

'How could they tell?' said Fiachra, bone dry, as ever, and he turned to a woman who had come up to him, with a squeal.

I don't know what she was like most of the time – Dahlia, or Delia, or Delilah – but at thirty-eight weeks' pregnant, she was as slow and hysterical as a turnip in a nervous breakdown. She pulled me in over her belly – literally pulled me by the cloth of my top – and said, in a low voice:

'Why is my husband talking to that girl?'

'What?' I said. 'Would you give over.'

'No really,' she said. 'Does he know her?'

She was crying. When did that start?

I said, 'Would you like something to eat, maybe?' and she said, 'Oh. Food.'

Like she had never thought of doing *that* before.

I sat her on a sofa and brought her a plate filled with everything: quiche, poached salmon, green salad, potato salad with roasted hazelnuts, a grated celeriac thing; also a few cuts of some bird, with sausage stuffing and some clovey, Christmassy, red cabbage. It wasn't catered, I noticed. They had done it themselves.

'It's a bit mixed up,' I said.

'Oh well,' she said. 'Never mind, eh?'

I wanted to get away from her, but it didn't seem possible. There was an equal temptation to sit beside her – for warmth almost – and I gave in to that instead, checking around me that Seán was once again out of the room. Or perhaps it was Conor I was worried about, even though I knew he was so far away.

She was wearing a red T-shirt over maternity jeans, with a little sequinned bolero that looked, against the scale of her breasts, like it had come off a Christmas toy. She balanced the plate of food on her bump, then hoisted herself more upright to place it on her knee. Finally she put the plate on the arm of the sofa, and twisted the less pregnant part of herself around to it, leaving the more pregnant part behind.

'Oh Christ.'

I thought I heard her whimper, as she started to eat; actually whimper. I turned to watch the room and the balloon of her stomach continued to swell in the corner of my eye.

'Oh Christ.'

Something moved across her belly, a ripple, or a shadow, and I startled the way you would for a spider or a mouse. I turned to stare and it happened again – what looked like a shoulder bone cresting and subsiding, like something pushing its way through latex, except it wasn't latex under there, it was skin.

Maybe it was an elbow.

'Dessert?' I said.

'God yes,' she said, without turning around. And I got up and left her, and failed to find her a dessert, or to feed her again.

It was the kind of party where no one ate the chicken skin. Glazed in honey as it was, with a hint of chilli, the chicken skin was left at the side of every plate. I discovered this later when I cleared some dishes out to the kitchen, slaloming between the guests, and humming as I went. I left them on the kitchen counter beside Seán, who tended his pot of hooch, and really, possibly, wished that I would go.

Or wished that everyone else would go. I couldn't quite tell.

'Good Christmas?' I said.

'Yes thanks,' he said. 'You?'

'Lovely.'

I had, besides, no intention of going. I was having too good a time.

Back at the buffet, Fiona and the Mummies were giving it all they had. They leaned in for scurrility, then reeled back with laughter, hands going to mouths, *Oh no!* People dodging sideways to scoop up a glass, or snaffle an extra piece of this or that. There were little bowls of glazed nuts, and dried mango slices that had been dipped in dark chocolate. Really dark. At least 80 per cent.

'Am I dead? Is this heaven?' a woman said across to me, before lifting her head with a loud,

'Fuck it, I knew her at school.'

They were talking about plastic surgery. Indeed, a couple of women in the room had the confused look that Botox gives you, like you might be having an emotion, but you couldn't remember which one. One had a mouth that was so puffy, she couldn't fit it over the rim of her wine glass.

'Someone get the woman a straw,' said the schoolfriend, and she turned to consider the sherry trifle, her hand lifting to the skin of her neck.

I recognised someone from the telly over by the far wall, and an awful eejit from the *Irish Times*. And of course Aileen had a job, I remembered now, she was some kind of college administrator – which explained the academic types in their alarming clothes, who hogged all the chairs and watched the room with stolid eyes. The Enniskerry husbands stood about and talked property: a three-pool complex in Bulgaria, a whole Irish block in Berlin. Seán wasn't working the room, so much as playing it. He went about seeding slow jokes, glancing back for the bellow of laughter.

'Don't worry,' he threw over his shoulder. 'I'll invoice you for that in the morning!'

Aileen, too, was on her mettle. She caught me in the kitchen doorway, and asked me lots of interesting questions about myself. Slightly lit up, as she was, a champagne flute in her hand, she quizzed me about my life. 'Where are you living now?' And she was so cheery and bright, she had everything so much under control, it was – I am not wrong about this – like a fucking interview. For what job? Who knows.

I didn't care.

I had a few too many glasses of white under my belt, and a ring on my finger; a big plastic fake rock from my mother's dancing days, that might have been made of Kryptonite. I could go upstairs and leave a kiss on his pillow, or a lychee – they had some, I noticed, in the turned-wood fruit bowl. I could stay too long in the upstairs bathroom and have a good snoop: olive-green walls, smelly candle, weather-beaten wooden buddha to watch, and bless perhaps, all the excretions of the house. There was a white lattice cupboard under the sink, where various products lurked: I could steal a squirt of his wife's perfume, or just take the name for later (ew, though, White Linen?). What words should I write on the mirror, to show up later in the steam of the shower? In what corner might I dribble my spit? The cupboards were flush, the floorboards tight, but there might be a gap or crack somewhere, where a hex of mine might rot, or grow:

Seán, where did this thong come from? The one under the bed?

Though this dark magic, surely, could work against you too.

The room where they slept was white. Or near white. The ceiling was cut by the slope of the eaves and it was done in horribly similar, crucially different shades of fucking white. I mean I didn't have the colour chart in my hand, but it was an old house, so let's give Aileen the benefit of posh here; let's call it bone white on the floorboards, the walls strong white, the wardrobe French white – that horrible furniture you get with the garlands and curlicues – and all surrounding the crisp white sheets, on the froth of a duvet, that fluffed itself up off their five-foot wide bed.

They had very few things.

In a way, that was what I envied most. No dressing gown on a hook, no shoes under the bed.

I tipped a door in the wall and it opened on the en-suite: many fitted cupboards, pin lights, a large shower-stall with a flat rose like the bottom of a bucket and, for extra clean, a second, smaller shower head at hip height.

Who could leave all that?

I went back on to the landing and listened.

The noise downstairs continued, indifferent to the silence where I stood, in the dead centre of the house. In the spare room, the bed was dark with heaped and waiting coats. Across the landing was the lavender glow of Evie's room, that hummed, in the dusk, almost ultraviolet. It too, was perfect. A dream-catcher by the window, a little white bed. The door was open, I did not have to pry. I was looking for the distinctive thing, tacky or sweet, as a sign of the girl herself; something scabbed or plastic, like the dinosaur stickers my niece had put on her bedroom door that no one had the energy to remove. But there was nothing. I mean, there was nothing there that I could identify. It was only a glance.

I heard something though, as I turned to leave; a terrible, soft noise, guttural and broken – and definitely human, though it sounded like a cat was dying, very quietly, behind the door. I was about to back away when I remembered the child had fits, and so I found myself stuck there, trying to do the right thing, while the little, broken mewlings continued. Up and then down. And then up again. And down.

She was singing. It wasn't a fit, it was a song. I put my head around the door in pure relief and there she was, sitting on the floor, with a big set of Bose headphones over her ears, crooning along.

She dragged the headphones off as soon as she saw me. She even tried to hide them, behind her back.

'You're all right,' I said. *God, what a house.*

'My Mum doesn't like it,' she said.

'Right.'

'She says it makes me look stupid.'

'Really?' I said, keeping things cheerful.

'You have no idea,' she said, complicit, almost camp. *The things I have to put up with.*

I laughed.

'Did you hear about the magic tractor?' I said.

'No, what?'

'It went down the lane and turned into a field.'

She rolled her eyes.

'What age are you, anyway?'

'Like – nearly ten?'

'Ah well,' I said. 'That's soon cured.'

'Are you looking for your coat?'

'Not yet,' I said.

'It's in the au pair's room,' she said, hopping up to show me anyway. Fortunately, there were other people coming to get their things: three men, the bulk of them filling the staircase from banister to wall. I had to wait until they were past before I could make my way downstairs.

IN MY ABSENCE, the party had shifted up a gear. You can never catch the moment when it happens, but it always does:

that split second when awkwardness flowers into intimacy. This is my favourite time. Those who were drinking had drunk too much, and the ones who were driving had ceased to matter. I got another white wine and floated through the room on a beautiful sea of noise; ended up slap bang against my brother-in-law, who bellowed at me that he had spent three years on the old-fashioned anti-depressants before he met my sister.

'Just to take the edge off, you know?'

Well I didn't know. My brother-in-law is an engineer. He gets really uptight about health and safety on his construction sites, and this is as much insight into his emotional life as I need, thank you.

'I was pretty stuck with it,' he said. 'Three years, you know?'

'I can imagine.'

Seán swung past with a bottle of white.

'Are you drunk?' he said, quietly.

'Not really.'

'Well, why the hell not?' he shouted, and slopped some more into my glass. Then he did the same for Shay.

'Shay my man, she's a relative!'

'Please,' said Shay, holding up an innocent hand.

'What? You think you got the better deal?' said Seán. Then he turned back to me with a wink.

It was an interesting tactic, flirting with someone you had no need to flirt with anymore. I could see the logic of it. Though I thought, also, his eyes were a little wild.

Evie had come downstairs. I saw her shifting from foot to foot, in front of one of the academic types; an old man, who reached out to take the cloth of her blouse between thumb and finger.

'Come here to me a minute.'

I wanted us all to be sober for her: *What age are you now?* She wriggled and itched, and looked like she loved it too. Awful as it was to be noticed by these people (they're nothing much, I wanted to shout over to her, they are no great shakes) she smiled and rolled her eyes to the wall, until her mother came to release her. Aileen set her hands on Evie's shoulders, letting the child slip away from under them, and she disappeared among the adults, leaving a disturbance of lifted glasses, as she made her way across the room.

Every time I saw her father, meanwhile, he was flirting with someone. It looked harmless, because Seán wasn't tall. The way he leaned in, it made him look, as he teased one woman or engaged in serious conversation with her husband, merely friendly. But it never stopped. I noticed that, too. The way he put his hand on the small of every woman's back, so they could feel the warmth of it there.

I couldn't be jealous. In the circumstances, that would be a bit silly.

Besides, his wife didn't seem to mind.

I met her again in the hall, when Fiona was trying to head home and there was fuss about arrangements.

'Oh don't you go too!'

She touched my arm. She seemed – I am looking for the right word here – *fond* of me. As though there was something about me that made her nostalgic and hopeful, something that gave her a pang.

'Seán can walk you back, whatever happens. Won't you Seán?'

'Sorry?' He was standing inside the big room, with his back to us.

'Walk Fiona's sister down the road.'

'What?'

'Don't worry,' I said. 'As I keep telling my sister here, I am getting a lift back into town with Fiachra.'

Because Fiachra and his Fat Flower were at their last party ever – they might as well have brought their pyjamas. She had already taken one little nap on the sofa and had woken up for more.

I waved my sister and her husband away from the door and knew, as they walked into the country darkness, that it was not wise to stay. I watched them as far as the gate; Fiona tiny beside the bulk of her husband, reaching over to take his hand. Then I turned to Aileen and said, 'Those mango slices are a crime!'

I HAD JOINED SEÁN and Fiachra as they hovered near his sleeping wife.

'First year – no sex,' Fiachra was saying into his wine glass. 'Isn't that what they say?'

'Ah, stop it,' said Seán. 'You won't know yourselves.'

Behind us, the woman slept, while the baby – I don't know – smiled, or sucked its thumb, or listened and knew better, while, on the back of the sofa, the side of Seán's hand touched the side of mine. I could feel the thick fold in the flesh, at the bend of the knuckles. And it was surprisingly hot, this tiny piece of him. That was all. He did not move, and neither did I.

But once we had begun, how were we supposed to stop? This sounds like a simple question, but I still don't know the answer to it. I mean that we had started something that could not be ended, except by happening. It could not be stopped, but only finished. I mean the woman with the chocolate-dipped mango who was eyeing up the sherry trifle, and the boys with the Bulgarian complex that had three whole Bulgarian pools, two in the garden and one on the roof, and everyone with a last drink who was thinking about another last drink, and me sitting with my hand touching the side of Seán's hand in his own house – we were all drunk, of course, but I could no more have left it at that than Fiachra's baby could have decided to stay where it was for another couple of years. I could no more ignore it than you could ignore the smell of the sea at the road's end – turn back without checking that the water was there and that it was wide.

Our reflections rolled and flickered over the flawed old glass of the four long windows, with all the loveliness of Christmas past and for a moment it was as though everything had already happened. We had loved and died and left no trace. And what it wanted, what the whole world wanted, was to be made real.

The minute Fiona left, I made my way to the kitchen, with a blagged cigarette in my hand. Seán was there, opening a bottle of red.

'What's that?' he said.

'Is this the way out?'

'Don't,' he said.

I looked down at the cigarette and said, 'Oh for God's sake.'

I made my way to the sink, turned on the tap and drowned the thing, then opened the cupboards under the sink, one door after another, and threw it in Seán Vallely's own, personal, domestic bin. After which, I straightened up and looked at him.

'Wow,' I said. 'I love your units. What are they, oak?'

'Something like that,' he said.

And I wandered back into the fray.

It was getting to that time when everyone is unspooled and sad to be leaving, though they never actually do leave; the hour when bags are lost and taxis fail to arrive. It was the lost hour, the hour of unravelling intentions, and it was in this extra time, while Aileen hunted in the living room for Dahlia's abandoned shoes, that I kissed Seán, or he kissed me, upstairs.

It was Fiachra's fault. I have never been at an event with Fiachra which he has left voluntarily. Drunk or sober, he is the kind of guy who has to be dragged backwards through life. I offered to get the coats, just to move things along, and was halfway there when I heard Seán take the stairs behind me, saying, 'I'm on to it.' He followed me across the landing, and I made it into the au pair's room before turning around.

I had expected – I don't know what I had expected – some kind of collision. I had expected lust. What I got was a man who looked at me through pupils so open and black, you could not see the iris. What I saw, when I turned, was Seán.

I kissed his mouth.

I kissed him. And as kisses go it was almost innocent; a second too long, perhaps. Maybe two. And at the beginning of that extra second I heard Evie squeaking at the sight of us; towards the end of it, her mother's voice downstairs.

'Evie! What are you doing up there?' making the child glance back over her shoulder, as my eyes rolled, a little comically, towards the door.

Seán pulled away. He took a breath. He held me at the hips. He said: 'Happy New Year!'

I said, 'Happy New Year to you, too!' and Evie's hands began to flap as she lifted her arms from her sides.

'Happy New Year!' she said, and she barrelled into her father. 'Happy New Year, Daddy!'

He bent to kiss her too; a peck on the lips, and she encircled him with her arms and squeezed tight, and tight again.

'Hoofa! Ooofa!' said her father.

Then she turned to me.

'Happy New Year, Gina!' she said.

And she tilted her face up, so I could kiss her too.

The coats were gathered and Evie preceded us down the stairs. She put a soft white hand on the banister and walked carefully in front of us, one sock drifting towards her ankle, a row of corrugations around her calf where the elastic left its red reminder, her hair a little dishevelled, her cheek, as I knew from kissing it, sticky with stolen sugar. She had sneaked a go of the White Linen, but, from under her clothes, came the tired smell of a body that is not yet sure of itself. She seemed so proud; like a little herald, full of news beyond her understanding.

The front door was open and Dahlia stood on the doorstep

facing the night, while Fiachra lingered inside the living room, draining a final glass. As we came down the stairs, the pregnant woman stretched her arms above her head. She looked a little fat, from behind; her spine curved back on itself, beautiful and sturdy, while her hidden belly lifted to the sky.

She dropped her hands.

'Home' she said, and turned around to me. 'Are you right, so?'

Aileen obliged Fiachra into the hall, then she put coats on the parents-to-be and she kissed them both. Then Seán kissed them. Then Seán kissed me on the cheek, his hands pushing simultaneously at my shoulders, so it wasn't so much a kiss as a kind of bounce back from each other. Then Aileen gave me a hug, and stood back to look at me. She put an admiring hand on my hair, just over my ear, and she said, 'You must come again soon,' and I said, 'Yes.'

'And Donal too.'

'Conor.'

'Yes,' she said. 'Goodnight. Goodnight!' and she watched, silhouetted in the doorframe with her lovely husband and her lovely daughter, as we got into the car and drove away.

'God,' said Fiachra, slipping down in the passenger seat in front of me, while his wife grunted at the gearshift.

'God almighty. Out of there I thought we Would Not Get.'

I HAVE THOUGHT ABOUT IT a lot, since – how much Aileen did or did not know. When it all blew up in our faces, Seán said that she had been 'in denial'. He said 'you have no idea' (*the things I have to put up with*). They must realise, these women.

They must, on some level, know what is going on. I know it sounds like a harsh thing to say, but I think we should own up to what we know. We should know why we do the things that we do. Otherwise it's just a mess. Otherwise we are all just flailing around.

When Conor came in the door the next day, sometime after noon, he looked at me, lying on the sofa with a sleeping bag thrown over me, watching 'The Simpsons' with the remote in my hand. He said, 'Where's the car?'

THE SHOOP SHOOP SONG (IT'S IN HIS KISS)

AFTER THE PARTY, things went quiet for a while. There was something too intimate there, that did not suit us – or did not suit me. I had flashbacks to the top of the stairs and, in the whiteness, I seemed to grow and shrink as I reached out my hand to open Seán's bedroom door. I'd startle back to myself to find the taxi man still complaining, or some meeting called to an unsatisfactory conclusion while I sat on, my files scattered in front of me.

'See you Tuesday.'

'Yes. Yeah sure.'

It wasn't just me. There was a lull in the beginning of that year; a sense of in-taken breath. The boss was in Belize, of all places, looking at a villa. Fiachra's baby refused to arrive. Seán's report was not due until the first of February, but nobody seemed wild about Poland anymore. I don't know how it translated into euros and cents, I just remember it as a mood; how Warsaw, whose streets I had so recently walked, became as foreign to me as it had been when I did not know their word for Thursday and never knew I might want to. Who would have thought, growing up as a nice Irish girl, that this language would give me such pleasure? And those Polish men, my goodness, so proud and sexy as they bowed – some of them actually did do this – to kiss my outstretched hand. I mean, I nearly bought a flat there. But even then, in January 2007, it had started to go a bit cabbage-shaped. Outside the window, the day refused to stretch. Even the planet was taking its time.

One day towards the middle of the month, I answered my mobile to a withheld number and Seán was on the other end, as I knew he would be; everything to play for in the silence after he said, 'Hi.' And also nothing. I was ready – I have always been ready – just to walk away.

'Hello,' I said.

'When can I see you?' he said.

The pain I felt was so sudden and unexpected, it was like being shot. I looked down the length of myself, as if to share the news with my body, or to check that it was all still there.

We went to the Gresham again. Seán paced the room, he said, 'We need somewhere. Jesus.'

I caught him from behind and put my face against his back. I reached for his hands and crossed them over his stomach, as if to reassure him that the party was over, as Christmas was over, that whatever happened – if anything had actually happened – was something out of time.

But he was fierce and preoccupied and lay afterwards staring at the ceiling. He put his hands over his face, and pushed them up and over his eyes, which opened again as soon as he was done.

If I had a picture of that time of our lives it would be this:

Seán's face disappeared under his hands, his neck red to the collarbone, and the rest of his body strangely white. There is more if I want to think about it: the sepia blush of his private parts, the condom slack and yellow, his chest hair turning white. Or I can see his hands, which I loved, square tipped and intelligent, his eyes beneath them grey as a January sea.

He shifted over on to his side and stroked my face. He said, 'You're lovely, you know that?'

I said, 'You're not so bad yourself.'

SEÁN FILED HIS REPORT and the boss took it off home with him and nothing more happened; it might as well not have been written.

And so it went. Winter refused to shift into spring, and for a while it seemed as though we knew what we were doing. We met every second Friday and sometimes, if he could manage it, the Friday in-between.

At first, I chose my clothes with great care. But we were so seldom dressed; after a while I just wore things that would not get too creased when they ended up on the floor.

There is something so open about a hotel bed, the duvet kicked away; it was like a plinth, or a padded stage, and the shapes we made there were more sweet and anguished for seeming abstract, as we fitted together our jigsaw love, one way, or another, ending up one evening at dusk, with me spooned around the curl of his body on the bare sheet; his eyes, when I lifted my head to check, burning with the impossibility of it all.

When I think of those hotel rooms, I think of them after

we left, and only the air knew what we had done. The door closed so simply behind us; the shape of our love in the room like some forgotten music, beautiful and gone.

After we made love – which we always did first, for fear, almost, of becoming friends – afterwards, when it was safe, Seán would talk to me about his life and I would be interested, looking at him beside me, dazed by the details. The corner of his mouth, for example, which was the precise location of his charm. This was where it happened; at the point where his lower lip doubled back from the upper, the angle – I had kissed it – where they divided and met. In its slow lift, the charm of a smile you do not trust, and like all the more for that.

Seán did not talk about Evie, or about his wife. He did not mention the house in Enniskerry, or the house overlooking the beach in Ballymoney, though he was happy to talk about anything else. More than happy. Seán loves to chat and I love to chat, and there were times when we caught hold of ourselves for getting on too well. It was in no one's interests (we both knew this) to have that kind of a good time.

We stayed until dark and each time the dark came later.

When Seán was young, he told me, he had a red setter that would feck eggs from a local hen-house and his mouth was so soft, he could run back home without cracking the shell.

He talked about Boston where he did his MBA. Two years in America makes you an outsider for the rest of your life, he said: coming home was so strange, it was like arriving in from a long walk on a beautiful autumn day to find everyone still huddled around the fire.

He told me about his family: an older brother who annoyed

him for no exact reason – he had blown this brother out of the water, anyway, and this made him a bit sad. Winning was a lonely occupation for Seán – though that never seemed to stop him. The brother was a secondary-school teacher who thought Seán was a snob. Seán said he was anything but – he thought snobbery bad for business – but still the brother used to say, *So how're the ghastly middle classes*, and borrow things that he never returned; box sets, a cast-iron cooking pot, a buoyancy aid from the kayak down in Ballymoney. The brother was also, I discovered when I finally met him, six foot two, with a smile that curled up, not just on one side, but on the other too; he was Seán on steroids, and gentle with it. I thought, when he looked at me in his lovely, disappointed way, that now would be a good moment to go to the nearest convent, if such a thing still existed, and take the veil – I mean, *on my knees* – that man was so sexy, he was the point of no return.

Anyway. According to Seán, there was this useless older brother, with his chain-store jackets and his fat wife. There was also a younger sister, much loved, who was an artist down in Kilkenny. There was a father some years dead, and a mother who was very much alive. I couldn't tell what the problem with the mother was, except it was clear that the wrong parent had died. The way he talked, you'd think she had actually done it; slipped something into her husband's tea, or taken a pillow to his sleeping face; the mere fact of her was enough to put the man in an early grave.

And this was interesting, because for the Moynihan girls – and this was our dirty little secret – it was the right parent who had died. Myself and Fiona might fall out over his memory from time to time – we would argue what he was, or was not (violent, for example; Fiona would say, 'He was never *violent*'), but there was no doubt that we felt easier about the world, for the fact that our father was no longer in it. We loved him, of course, but we both knew that life was simpler now that he wasn't just 'out', or 'late', or even 'gone on a wander', but definitely and definitively dead, dead, dead. No coming back. No late-night key scratching for the lock.

I don't think I told Seán all that much about him, though he was quite interested in the lives we led after Daddy died: the Moynihan women, all dressed in black. He really liked the sisters thing, he wanted – I don't know – teenage details; snogging at the corner, disasters with underwear. He liked the idea of us growing up; myself and Fiona causing a stir, as he put it, in the pants of every boy in Terenure.

He talked about his mother quite a lot. I mean, it was clear I would never have to meet this woman, he could say whatever he liked. I would not have to listen – the way you do – to tales of tenderness or brutality, and then shake some old woman's hand, to discover that she was quite ordinary, really: a bit dimmer than you expected, or sharper, but surprisingly faded and human, though not always – as I recall from other women I have heard described by naked men – entirely nice. Anyway, he told me about his mother, the way Conor used to do and before that, Fergus, and before that, Axel from Trondheim, who called his mother 'Meen Moooor' and before that various others, though my virgin years were mostly spared. After sex, that is when men talk about their mothers; before sex they are a little affronted by the mention of her. As for daughters; my experience of sleeping with fathers is limited, but I suspect that daughters are only discussed when everyone is fully dressed. Daughters are discussed in the morning light. Or they are not discussed at all. I mean that they are completely irrelevant and completely forbidden, both at the same time.

Don't go there.

OK. Fine.

But I am becoming distracted from the subject of Margot, Seán's mother, the bank manager's wife and Sunday painter, who drank an actual martini every day at half past five, and was not a beauty, though she considered herself to have an Interesting Face.

'Thin?' I said.

'As a rake,' he said. 'Hands like,' and he made the same swirl and grab of the air, that I had seen and loved, that time in Montreux.

'Of course,' I said.

Seán's mother needed space to grow as an artist and a human being, and Seán's father moved around every few years on his way up the ladder of the Bank of Ireland, so Seán was packed off to boarding school at the age of twelve – and not a posh boarding school, at that, but the kiddy-fiddlers down in Wexford, where they beat the shit out of you, and didn't even bother to teach you French.

But the school was fine – no one touched him, one way or the other – there was nothing terribly wrong with the school. It was the mother and her daubings, that was the problem; it was Margot and her 'needs'. The day he got his exam results she decided it was time that she too went to college, and he spent the entire summer dreading UCD where his mother, as he thought, would be holding court in a corner of the student bar. In the event, she decided on art college instead, then changed her mind and wanted to study counselling.

'And did she?'

'Did she what?' said Seán. 'Did she *shite*.'

I thought she sounded quite interesting in a way. I was almost sorry I would never look her in the eye. Or that, if I did look her in the eye, she would not know who I was:

'What wonderful watercolours, Mrs Vallely. Don't tell me you did them all yourself.'

THE AFFAIR, AS I HAD LEARNED to call it, progressed in its Friday pace. The sex became less filthy and more fun, the silence filled with talk – laughter even – and this unsettled me. I might have preferred silence. Every normal thing he said reminded me that we were not normal. That we were only normal for the twelve foot by fourteen of a hotel room. Outside, in the open air, we would evaporate.

I bumped into him one evening in March. I was with a client, a plastics guy from Bremen, with a Plattdeutsch accent like someone walking in shoes three sizes too big for him. It was not a glamorous evening. We ended up in Buswells for a nightcap and there was Seán with some suits in the corner, being the thing – the way men can do that, somehow – making money just by being himself.

I took a long route to the ladies in order to pass near him, and we had a funny, offhand little exchange. There he was. Dressed. Polite. He asked about work. I answered him.

He turned back to the suits and I went on to the toilets, where I started to shake so badly I could not open my bag to get a brush. I stood for a moment, trying to breathe. Then I washed my hands, and dried them carefully, with the little white towel. I touched the mirror where my face was, I pressed quite hard on the glass, then I went back in to my plastics man.

I was thirty-two. I remembered that fact, as I sat back down and looked about me. Apart from the waitresses, I was the youngest person in the room.

After the Buswells incident, I became petulant, hard to manage, and so we played that game for a while; the mistress game. He bought me a Hermès scarf – I mean, I am not a Hermès kind of girl – he produced it from behind his back after we kissed, like a man in a fifties film, and I said, 'Did you keep the receipt?'

A fortnight later, he produced a bottle of perfume from the same magical spot. It was a light, harmless kind of scent called Rain, and indeed it smelled a little of the rain, starting soft and warm on your skin (is there a perfume called Skin, I wondered), then opening to an afterwash of fresh air. I liked it well enough, though the end note was a bit like that chemical waft you get from tumble dryer sheets, that is supposed to remind you of clothes hung out on the line.

I set it down on the bedside locker but Seán picked it up again and sprayed some on the back of my neck before undressing me and the sex afterwards was hard to judge, somehow; a little intense and laboured on his part and, on mine, distracted at every turn by the artificial smell of rain in the room.

'Rain,' I said. 'What made you buy that?'

'I just thought you'd like it.'

'I do,' I said.

I am not a fake sort of person, but afterwards, in the smell of fabric freshener and sad, rainy days, I traced the lines around his eyes, and said, in a way that sounded fake, even to me,

'Have you done this before?'

It was the perfume that maddened me.

'Done what?'

I am not the kind of woman who wears Rain.

'All this. Have you done it before?'

'Well, you know,' he said.

When we met the next week, I wore my black suede boots with the fringe down the back seam, and I sat in the chair and crossed my legs and told him it was time to make an end. And after he agreed, and seduced me, and I resisted and then cried (just a little), he told me about the other girl, the first one. She was someone at work, he said. She was someone he had actually hired, at work, so go figure, but unbelievably it did not occur to him, except in a 'wouldn't mind' sort of way, and anyway he wasn't . . .

'What?' I said.

He just wasn't free. That was the bottom line. But something about her, slowly, something about her just broke him, the way she was, she had a thing for nail varnish, these tiny hands and her nails were done in all these bubblegum colours, they looked like sweets.

'And?' I said.

Well she was twenty-two, which, you know, looks great, but it was the emotion that sideswiped him, it came from nowhere. And she was twenty-two. So he was in love – he thought he was in love – and he had forgotten how it is at that age but she was really hard work. She wasn't thick, exactly – she still, God knows, went on about her B in Honours Maths – but she gave a very good impression of thick, talking about herself all the time, obsessing about her thighs, throwing things at him if he said the wrong, nice thing about her thighs.

And she couldn't take her drink, so it was always a mess, she was always maundering on about her mother or her horrible father, who turned out to be a guy Seán knew, actually, and she was fighting with taxi men and roaring in the street, so she had him by the balls, this crazy woman, he couldn't even sack her, he couldn't take the risk. And when it was finally over, he thought: so that's it. That was his chance, his fling. That was his big romance.

I waited for the next line.

'Until I met you.'

And we made love for a second time. I was very upset, although I did not show it. I was upset because I felt so lonely, all the way through.

I had taken to ringing his home number at night, and this was a disastrous thing to do. Disastrous to want it so badly; the sound of his voice in the middle of a long fortnight, although it might not have been his voice exactly I was looking for. This was me ringing the landline to Enniskerry, the one I had seen nesting on the console table in the hall, and on the kitchen wall, and by the marriage bed. It was answered somewhere in the ordinary life of the house: Aileen with bleach foaming on her upper lip, Evie at the kitchen table, doing her homework,

Seán, apparently, elsewhere. The second or third time, Aileen did not cut the connection. She waited, and the silences of her life filled the earpiece, as I heard the nearness of her breath, and she felt the nearness of mine.

I zipped my calves back into the boots, holding my legs high, one after the other, to avoid the fringe. Seán sat on the edge of the bed putting in his cufflinks. He was wearing a pink shirt, impossibly pale. His jacket was hung over the back of the chair. He did not mention the phone calls. He bent down to lace up his plain, black shoes.

He said, 'You should never do this with someone – you should never expose yourself to someone like this – unless they have a lot to lose.'

I RAN HOME TO HIM that day. I ran home to my husband, to his wise brown eyes that were not, in fact, wise, and to his big, warm body that had not kept me from the cold.

On Saturday night I cracked open a bottle of wine and we watched 'The Wire' on box set, and after that we drank another bottle, despite which I was numb, in his arms, with the thought of all I had lost: the movement of his hand was just a movement, his tongue was an actual tongue. I had killed it; my best thing. The guilt, when it finally hit, was astonishing.

DANCE ME TO THE END OF LOVE

IN THE MIDDLE OF APRIL Seán was guest speaker at some motivational golfing weekend in Sligo and we had two days together – I can't remember what lie I told before I got on the train – two days, and one whole night, to end the affair; to strangle it and beat it about the head, to throw it in a shallow grave and go home.

Seán picked me up at the station (Evie's fluffy earmuffs abandoned on the back seat), and brought me out to a hotel, far from the golfers, on the outskirts of town.

The hotel was actually a converted asylum, massive, and grey. There were two Gothic chapels on either end of the car park, one smaller than the other.

'Protestant and Catholic maybe,' said Seán. Or staff and patients. But I said it was men one side and women the other. We looked at them when we got out of the car and thought about it: stolen glances across the forecourt. It was all there: the sackcloth, the raving, thwarted love.

'Jesus,' said Seán. 'It's the County Home.'

Then we walked into reception and found ourselves in the middle of two different hen parties, one in black T-shirts with magenta-coloured feather boas, another in white T-shirts with a pink slogan on the front. The slogan said: 'Aunt Maggie is on the Farm'.

I turned to pull a face at Seán but he was gone. Disappeared. I couldn't see him anywhere. In my foolishness I spun around in the hotel foyer, and then back again while the hen parties milled around in front of the desk. I finally pulled out my phone, to find a text that said, 'Sign in. Send no, will fllw'.

Something, or someone, had spooked him. And so I queued, the only woman in the place who wasn't wearing pink, and I panicked about my credit card, which had my name on it, which would, one day, turn into a credit-card bill, and I thought how resentment is the one true opposite of desire.

The room was impossible to find. I had to walk miles of corridor, go up in one lift, and down in a different one. The walls were hung with paintings done to match the carpet; an increasingly sickening series of abstracts in cream and maroon that looked like they came out of the same two pots of paint; the inmates' revenge. The room was in fact in the old nurses' quarters: a separate, modern building connected by a walkway to the main hotel, with the feeling along the length of it of going from madness to your dinner, and back again. I didn't know if these ghosts were any easier to handle, as they crept with naggins of vodka in their white pockets to trysts with doctors or orderlies, or with patients who were handsome and sad. A swirl of magenta feathers danced over the carpet as I passed, while at the end of the corridor some ancient echo asked me what I thought I was doing out of bounds at that hour, and in those high heels.

When I got up to the room, Seán was already lurking by the door.

'How did you manage that?' I said.

'Manage what?' Apparently it was all easy to find, from the outside.

We made love as soon as we saw the bed and then wandered the rooms – it was actually a family suite with a living room and kitchenette: dark wood, stripy cushions. Seán looked different there, more domestic, and used.

It was the end, I knew that. I think we both knew.

That afternoon, we drove to Rosses Point and kissed on the beach. The tiny flesh of his lips in front of that great ocean and, when he opened his mouth, it was like diving in.

Driving back along the coast road, Seán swung in through the gates of a house with a For Sale sign outside.

'Just curious,' he said, as he went up the driveway, and we parked right in front of their lives, whoever these people were, in their eighties dormer with its lawn running down to the sea.

They had a trampoline in the garden, and a separate garage – it looked nicer than the house actually – with room for two cars.

A silhouette paused in front of the window: a woman, checking us out.

'Do you want to buy it?' I said.

'Do I want to buy it?' Which was another thing that

annoyed me about him, the way he liked to deadpan what I just said. 'Giving it the cold read' as he called it.

'Are you interested in buying the house?'

'Always, my love,' he said. 'Always.'

My love.

We stayed for five long minutes, maybe more. At one stage he got out of the car and walked to the gap between the house and the garage, assessing the view down to the sea. Then he walked towards the car, backwards, checking the gutters as he came.

'OK,' he said.

And we left the woman with her trampoline and her swing set, that did not have the grass rubbed away beneath it, and to her life by the sea.

I kept checking my phone. No one knew where I was, and I felt cut loose – abandoned almost. I spent the entire time I was there, fantasising the call; the one I might get from Conor; the one from my mother's mobile that I answer, only to hear a stranger's voice at the other end. In fact, no one missed me, or wanted me; the phone stayed dead. It was just Sligo working its voodoo as we slid along the lost lanes, in the flat plain between Ben Bulben and the sea.

At Glencar Lake, he recited Yeats to me, 'Come away oh human child, to the waters and the wild.' Then we parked beyond the waterfall, and he pushed his seat back, and there was something about him, the expansive way he sat, I knew he wanted me to get up to some badness, that this would be a treat, what with the scenery and the poetry and the fact that we were in his very own, very nice car. And I thought, this can not be true. This man can not want me to blow him, in daylight, in a public car park. This man *whoever he is*.

I opened the glove compartment and looked at the CDs.

'Guillemots! Is this yours?'

'Yeah,' he said.

And he drove back to the hotel too fast, where I failed to seduce him on my way to the shower and he failed to seduce me on my way out of it. And on it went. We risked a meal in town, and hated it. Then we came back and fought. I sat on the bed and cried. I said, 'Why are you so horrible to me?'

He paused. He walked to the window and pulled back the curtain to watch the darkness, or his own reflection in front of the darkness. Then he let the curtain drop.

'Gina,' he said slowly, like he was explaining something it had taken him a while to understand. 'We don't really know each other.'

Which didn't stop us acting like we did. We had four whole rooms to do it in, I could slam a cupboard door in the kitchenette, he could clear his throat while sitting on the side of the bed to undo his shoes. I could drink a glass of wine at the table while he shook out the newspaper on the sofa behind me. He could stand at the bedroom window and look out at the car park while I shifted through the stations on the remote control. We could move about like this: as though we had a claim on each other, as though we were intimate. But we were only playing at these things. I knew that too. The way we leaned or sat, or directed our gaze; the gestures and arrangements we made of ourselves: living room, bedroom, bathroom, hall. And then later when we went to bed, the same play with pillow and duvet, turning towards or away from each other, and even our breathing a kind of demonstration.

In the darkness, something gave.

Seán said his marriage was unbearable. Not over but 'unbearable'.

'You have no idea,' he said.

It reminded me of his daughter sitting on her bedroom floor and saying just that. 'You have no idea.' *The things I have to put up with.*

But we did not talk about his daughter, and when I offered to talk about Conor, that felt wrong, too.

We talked about Aileen. Of course. We talked about his wife – because that is the thing about stolen love, it is important to know who it is you are stealing from.

'You don't understand,' said Seán. But I did understand; the wrongness of his wife, whatever it was, and her inescapability. And to be honest, I was a bit fed up with his wife, who was always somehow *there.* A part of me was beginning to think she was probably quite a nice woman, that there was nothing appalling about her.

'She just. You know . . .'

'I know.'

We brought it to a close. We played at being in love or not being in love, and even the sex, when it finally happened, wasn't great, and in the morning, we packed up our things and went home.

At the train station, I sat in the car and said to him, 'No more.'

He closed his eyes briefly and said, 'No more.' And we didn't know whether to kiss or not, so I just got out, and he popped the boot and came round to get my bag like a taxi man. He said, 'Have a good journey,' and I said, 'Thanks.'

I had a window seat, I looked out over the countryside, the stone walls of Sligo giving way to Leitrim bog. When we crossed the Shannon I was in love with him. By Mullingar I thought, if I did not see him soon again, that I would surely die.

EV'RY TIME WE SAY GOODBYE

THREE WEEKS LATER, on the fifth of May, my mother collapsed, in the middle of the afternoon, and was taken by ambulance to Tallaght Hospital. Luckily – if you could call it luck – it happened when she was out of the house. She was near Bushy Park at the time, though what she was doing there was a bit of a mystery. Joan never went down to the park. She used to say it was too close by to bother with and that, after the first twenty years or so, she gave up feeling guilty about all that fresh air. But it was outside the park gates that she held on to the bonnet of a car and then sat down on the ground. We did not know whether she was going there or coming back, we heard about the car from a woman in one of the houses opposite, who told us the story after the removal to Terenure church. As well she might: it was a good story.

'I did not see her hit the ground,' she said. 'She was the other side of the car from me, and she just sank down. When I came out she was sitting there, with her legs straight out, for all the world like a toddler or a little child, and her lovely camel coat fanned out on the path behind her.'

This woman, who seemed to know who we were, and who my mother was, and all her different coats, wanted to hand me a phone.

I did not want to take it. I did not see why I should.

'I found it later, after the car was gone.'

We were pretty sure it was our mother's phone, though the battery was now flat and neither Fiona nor I had the heart to recharge it. It made us wonder how much Joan knew, or guessed – the strange trip she made towards the park and, just before she fell, the attempt at making a call. It made us wonder how scared she was; not just the moment she reached for the bonnet of a stranger's car, but in the hour before that, or the day. And if a day – then what? The same thought was in both our minds: our mother had been frightened for a long time – months, a year perhaps – she had been frightened, and we had not seen it, and now she was beyond our soothing.

It was the loss of her mobile that delayed everything, I think. The first I heard was a phone call from the duty nurse at ten o'clock that night, explaining that our mother had been taken to the hospital, and perhaps I would like to come in. I mean, the woman was dead, she was effectively dead, but this must be what they say to relatives in such circumstances. And I knew this and did not know it, at the same time.

So this might be why I did not ask what had happened, or how Joan was now. It was because I knew this nurse, with her competent, lovely-Irish-girl voice, would not tell me, and that would make me hate her.

'Certainly,' I said. 'I'll be there as soon as I can.'

And she told me the name of the ward.

Fiona rang as soon as I put down the phone.

That day was a Saturday, and though I might easily have had a few glasses of wine, I was, in fact, sober – I must have been on a diet – and for this I was grateful. For the fact that I knew exactly what was happening, felt every step I took along the fluorescent corridors of the hospital night, and into the room where she was all wired up and ready to go. Fiona arrived with Shay. He and Conor talked to a doctor outside the door. They got us coffee from a vending machine. People passed, now and then. There was the flabby ker-clack of a distant zimmer frame, a horrible, wet fit of coughing. We sat with her into the early hours.

I don't know if I hated my sister as she sat in the room a few feet away from me or loved her. Whenever I looked over at her she seemed bizarrely separate from me, and the wrong age.

She is tiny, Fiona. I outgrew her when I was eleven. I don't know how she got pregnant, with that child's pelvis, it seemed so wrong. Now there she was, her knee beside her white face, the heel of her boot hooked on to the edge of the chair. How are you supposed to sit, when your mother is dying; when your mother is, effectively, already dead? I sat the way Joan taught me to: shoulders straight, hands loosely laced in my lap, legs crossed and angled slightly, to maximise the length of thigh. Like an air hostess. That is the way I sat, as my mother died.

My mother was a great beauty, in her day; more beautiful than either of her daughters, and all her bones were slender and long.

Conor told us that the doctor would let her go whenever we were ready. He said this without looking at anyone. He said it after leaning forward in his chair and taking up Joan's hand, and laying the palm of it along his cheek, and then setting it back on the counterpane. I did not want him to touch her, actually, I did not want anything to happen. And I can't remember any further discussion about this matter, but at perhaps one o'clock in the morning, the doctor, or whatever he was, came in and touched my arm. He had beautiful, compassionate eyes. He told me his name, which was Fawad. Then he flicked a couple of switches – they didn't look like much – while a nurse took the tubes away. He touched my arm again before he left the room, and I was glad I had met him. I thought, perhaps absurdly, that he had a great soul.

That was 1 a.m. Joan lay there for another twenty minutes, breathing. Her beautiful face was a dark shade of blue, her lips purple with a rim of black, and her chin was all wrong, like the jaw had been dislocated. She wasn't happy.

At a twenty past one, a nurse asked us to leave, just for a few minutes. She suggested we go for a cup of tea and shut the door after us. I don't know what she did in there. There was a sound of suction, I thought, like that thing at the dentists, but no one mentioned this at the time, or afterwards, and when we went back in, Joan was herself again, pale – for all the world asleep – her breath coming in wisps, and her face wiser than I had seen it before. She looked very beautiful. Her face was turning into the idea of a face. Not quite the one I recognised. Not quite her own. It looked like a face that might become hers, if she ever woke up to claim it.

I think I was the last to realise that she was gone.

It was like waking up – the realisation, I mean – it happened slowly at first and then, somehow, all in retrospect. We were in a room together; we were all sitting in this room. I had an impulse to giggle. We didn't know what to do, or whether we should stay.

Conor got up and went out into the corridor and I thought he might be running away. In fact he was just looking after business. The nurse came back and, though she didn't ask us to leave, we knew we had lost possession of our mother, and of the room. We were not wanted here. The nurse said, 'Take your time. Take your time.'

I stepped up to the bed and said, quite loudly – I mean, I said it in a normal, conversational voice – 'I won't kiss you, my darling,' and I touched her warm hand and turned to leave.

Behind me, Fiona said, 'Oh the kids! The kids!' as though they had died too, despite the fact that they clearly had not died. And everything became ordinary again. It was a hospital corridor at night; flowers on the windowsills, somebody coughing, my sister, these two men pushing us through the gloom.

'Who's minding them?' I said.

'A woman down the road, Aileen Vallely. You know her; Missus Issey Miyake.'

And the men led us down the corridor to the nurse's station, where we stopped at the high desk, and wondered was there anyone who might tell us what was supposed to happen next.

II

CRYING IN THE CHAPEL

WE HAVE BEEN WAITING, all week, for the snow. The cold came first. The air thrilled to it. Even indoors, the rooms felt bigger, their edges seemed more clear. The whole country was in a tizz. There were thirteen accidents on the back roads of Leitrim, there was black ice in Donegal. On Tuesday we watched the snow closing London down, covering the Cotswolds, building on the rails of the bridge into Anglesey, and melting, as if to prove its stealth, in the grey Irish Sea. It was snowing in Britain; it would snow here too.

Yesterday morning, the light was softer, the walls seemed to have moved closer in. Seán got out of bed and opened the curtains on the back garden, as though he was looking for something and I caught it, then – unbearably faint – the high, sweet smell of approaching snow.

Seán said he didn't know you could smell snow. He gave me a 'crazy girl' look as he went out on to the landing and snapped the string on the bathroom light. I heard it bounce against the mirror, once, twice. Then a silence so complete he might have ceased to exist. I looked at the place where he had stood at the window, and noticed the frost flowering along the edges of the pane.

The place is freezing.

The duvet, at least, is light and thick. It is easy to slide my legs into the warmth he has left, to take his pillow and turn it over to the cool side, and add it to my own.

I lie there watching the familiar square of day, with its new edge of lace: our breath, the sweat of our bodies, gathered in a crystal fog, that grew overnight into fronds and florets of ice.

The room faces east. I know, as well as anything, the sparse dawn light, but the trees this morning are a denser green, the clouds are low and bruised with the colours of unshed snow.

I am back, through no fault of my own, in the house where I grew up. It is the fifth of February – twenty-one months, to the day, since my mother sat down on the path with her coat fanned out around her. And still there are rooms I can barely bring myself to open. Not that we are living here. We are just sorting things out. Seán, especially, is not living here, though it is nearly a year, now, since he washed up at the door. We are in between things. We are living on stolen time. We are in love.

Next door in the bathroom, Seán sighs and, after a waiting pause, starts to pee. There is another pause when he is finished, or seems finished. Then a last little rush; an afterthought. It worries me, this sense of difficulty, surely there should be nothing simpler than taking a leak? And I remember my own father leaning like a plank over the toilet bowl, his hand braced against that bathroom wall, the side of his face nuzzled into his arm. Waiting.

'God this place is cold,' says Seán's voice.

He flushes the toilet and then appears back in the room to lift a dressing gown from the hook on the door. The dressing gown is a plaid design in thick grey towelling, that smells like it needs to be washed. I mean, when it is cold, it smells like this. When it is warm, it smells of Seán.

He puts it on over his pyjamas of striped jersey cotton.

Even when it is not about to snow, Seán wears pyjamas in bed. It is a habit he got into, he says, after Evie was born – not that she is around to see, except at the weekends. Even so, he walks around decent, and the world rests uncorrupted, thank goodness, by his nakedness.

The slippers are brown leather mules that slap as he walks about the room. He roots through his gym bag and shakes his dirty gear into the laundry basket. He goes back to the bathroom to get his shower gel and a fresh towel and when the bag is zipped and done, he drapes a jacket over it. I have weaned him off the suits, but there is still something too perfect about his shirts. He sends them out, now, at enormous expense, after the morning when he took one out of the wardrobe and said, in a puzzled voice, 'Is there something wrong with the iron?'

So the shirts come out of the chest of drawers now, and the cardboard ends up in a heap on top of it, and the little pins end up on the floor.

'I'll get the man again,' I say.

'God it's fucking freezing,' he says, shuffling out of one leather slipper and then the other, as he drops the pyjama bottoms and, with a staggered hop, gets into his underpants.

'Jesus, Jesus, Jesus,' he says, while the radiator gives an intestinal groan and something judders, downstairs.

I don't mind if he wears pyjamas at the weekend. I don't mind if he wears pyjamas every night of the week. We are in love. He can wear what he likes. Even so, I wonder if there was a time when he walked this room naked; was there a day last summer, when I saw him silhouetted against the window light? Because the most foolish thing about Seán's bare flesh is its purity. And though I have lusted after him mightily, in my time, it was always about getting him to the point where his body is as simple as it wants to be; as cruel, or as easy. There is very little about it, I would have thought, to frighten a child.

'What am I thinking?' he says. 'I'm in Budapest.'

'Today?'

'Just tonight. Just to sort it out.'

'I don't mind,' I said.

He takes his trolley bag down from the top of the wardrobe, then changes his mind and puts an extra shirt into his gym bag, which he then takes out again.

'What am I doing? What am I doing here?'

'Where are you staying, the Gellert?'

'I can't face the Gellert,' he says.

I don't know if this is a compliment to me or not. We had a weekend there, sometime last year, before the arse fell out of the Hungarian forint. It seems a long time ago now. You could actually see Seán's apartment up the river, a row of three beautiful nineteenth-century windows on the far bank. He had rented the place out to a guy who claimed to be an importer of mobile phones – and maybe he was. He is, in any case, gone now, along with four months' unpaid rent. That long-ago weekend – just last year, as I say: August 2008, when everything was still to play for – Seán finished the paperwork and slapped the phone importer's back, and we went off to spend the afternoon down in the Gellert's hot springs. We paddled about the beautiful old pool, then went our separate ways: him to the naked men and me to the naked, mostly old, women, every shape and size of them, who groaned as they eased themselves into the gentle waters, or slapped it towards them in small waves, gathering solace. I don't think we made love in Budapest. We made money, of course, or Seán made money, but there was too much history downstairs, soaking in the hot pools and plunging into the cold. Too many sagging thighs and bald pubic mounds and yellow stomachs, with their stretch marks of ancient silver. In the middle of it all were two California Girls, with water up over the tips of their beautiful fake breasts, who looked about them appalled; like this is all so wrong, there must be someone they could sue.

Or we thought Seán was making money. It turns out he was actually losing money. But you know, it still felt good.

I don't think he liked the baths, though. 'Talk about *Midnight Express*,' he said – meaning that Turkish prison movie from the seventies. We talked all evening, and we stayed too late in the hotel bar, and he fell asleep still holding the remote control.

'There's an Ibis out by the airport.'

He has a third bag now, hauled out from the bottom of the wardrobe, a knock-off Bally he got in Shanghai. The bed is covered with luggage.

'No, don't do that,' I say. 'Stay in town.'

And he stands there, looking at it all.

'Jesus, it's cold.'

He slaps over to the wardrobe and comes back to the bed empty-handed. Then he grabs his clean gear out of the gym bag and says, 'Fuck it, I'll just come back.' And he starts to put the tracksuit on.

Seán's legs are white. The hair has rubbed away from his shins and calves – not a thing I would have noticed, until I saw him one day in front of the mirror, craning around to check, like a woman with crooked seams.

'I'll do a quick gym.'

'Good luck.'

'I'll be back in a bit.'

'I'm gone too,' I say. 'Dundalk.'

'Don't make me jealous.'

He kisses me, quickly, as I lie there in the bed.

'If we make it, either of us, through the snow,' I say.

And he goes. No breakfast. The scrape of the garage door, with his bicycle being pushed through it.

An empty space in front of a window. A wilderness on the glass, of encroaching ice. The smell of snow.

I AM LATE, MYSELF, now. I lie there for a second, then another second, and am out from under the duvet and into the bathroom before he has joined the flow of traffic on Templeogue Road.

I twist the knob on the shower and go to brush my teeth while the water warms, turning the light on over the mirror.

Rrr-chink.

That string – the little plastic doo-dah at the end of it is chipped, and the string is knotted underneath to hold it on –

it is eating itself with knots, crawling higher up the wall, and the twine itself is dense with whatever is left by twenty, thirty years of human fingers, as we approach that mirror, and pull it down. Rrr-chink! I am so intimate with the sound of it, and the silence that follows as we acknowledge the image that meets us in the glass, and allow it, a little grudgingly, to be ourselves.

Remember me?

No.

The cleanest place in the house, that mirror; the way it refuses to hold the past. I leave it to the blank contemplation of the far wall, step into the shower-stall, and drag the door closed: the same metal pipe squirting water at its base, the same shower head. New water though; nice and hot.

The towel, with a pattern of pink roses and mint-green leaves, is nearly as old as I am, and still soft. But most of the family stuff is gone, and I rarely use what is left of it. We sleep in Fiona's old room, which seems a little odd – but less odd, somehow, than my childhood bed, which is next door to my mother's old bed, which was once my father's bed too. The spare room is for Evie. So we make love in this one place, the rest of the house remains inviolate. I take up only two drawers in the chest of drawers, and Seán takes the other two. We live on the sound of my mother's old radio, our laptops, one clapped-out TV. We leave very little trace.

This is, surprisingly, easier for Seán who would rather have nothing than the wrong thing – and this is part of his snobbery too.

'Don't be such a snob,' I say.

'Why not?' he said once and I said, 'It's so ageing.'

I love Seán. I am in love with Seán. I only punish him to keep him by my side. The cufflinks are gone, the Ray-Bans are forgotten in the glove compartment. He cycles into work now, his iPod playlist is a joy to behold. And in the middle of the night I help him kick off the pyjamas. I place my foot between his thighs and push them down.

The empty bedroom makes me want him again. I go to the wardrobe and pick out something he likes, even though he will not see me wearing it. I take his perfume from the bedside locker – the gift of rain – and grab the laundry basket on my way downstairs.

Halfway down, I step over some version of myself; a girl of four or six, idling or playing in the place most likely to trip people up. This is where children sit, I know this now; how they love doorways, in-between places, the busiest spot. This is where they go vague and start to dream.

Oh for God's sake.

My mother's shoes are some posh colour that is hard to name; sable, or taupe. Her arms are full of clean clothes.

DOWNSTAIRS, IN THE KITCHEN, I go about on her familiar track and I find it all comforting and sad; the jolt in the neck of the tap as the water hits; the aimless click of the ignition waiting for the gas to light.

Whomp.

The washing machine is the new one she bought, after the old one that gave her so much trouble. I know she found it hard to build up a full load. A lot of her stuff was dry clean only; it is possible, in that last year, that the machine was not much used.

Or so I thought when I opened the wardrobe in her bedroom and caught the thin, sour smell of abandoned clothes.

'Old age doesn't smell much,' she said once, in her arch way. And she was right. But it does smell a little.

It was some time before we opened the cupboards and the drawers. Shay said nothing could be touched for two weeks – something to do with probate, though I am sure we left it for nearly four. A month at least, to let the place fade a little, before we could begin to dismantle her life; divvy it up and throw it away. Then the surprise to find that it had not actually faded. All her things were just as she had them; bright and clean and particular. It was too hard. She liked all that Scandinavian stuff and I brought it back from my travels: a reindeer holding candles in its antlers, paper stars I bought in Stockholm, a beautiful wooden platter. The place was frayed at the edges, of course, the flooring a little clapped out, the fittings and fixtures, as the estate agents have it, *in need of renewal.* But she painted the rooms in those floating northern colours between blue and green: aqua, Pale Powder, Borrowed Light. She did it herself, the lines were not quite true. I wonder why she didn't get the painters in and where the money went: school fees, college, Armani jackets. All fur coat and no knickers, that's the Moynihans for you, though when you think about it, the home-improvements thing didn't happen until recently. Fiona, who for weeks at a time sees more of her plumber than her husband – that's all new.

We went in together, to clear her things away. We met at the corner and walked down, as we used to do from school. Fiona is, in fact, the same weight she was in sixth year, though motherhood has settled in her gait and her hair colour has brightened over the years from mouse-brown to a more glamorous afghan-hound.

I don't know what I looked like. If you asked me my age, in the weeks after Joan died, I would not have been able to say. I seemed to shift from hour to hour around some heavy, unchanging thing. I felt ancient. I felt like a child.

We looked to each other, at the front door. Fiona deferred and I put my version of the key in the lock, and we walked in to the smell of our childhoods, and the bright, neat hall.

We didn't, in fact, sort Joan's things. We went, as though by agreement, to our old bedrooms at the back of the house, and we sorted our own. I had a roll of bin bags and I filled two of them with fluffy toys, books, belts, beads and shoes. Only a mother could love this tat, I thought, wondering what Joan saw when she looked at this faded plastic – some happiness of her own, some childhood, that was not quite my childhood. I had lost this too.

I knotted my bags and left them on the landing, ready for the skip. Fiona took hers with her out to the car.

'You're not going to hang on to all that?' I said. And she said, No, she would take them home and throw them out there.

'Right,' I said.

It was hard, after that first occasion, to find a suitable time. Between Megan's maths homework and Jack's eczema, Fiona just could not get away. I was busy at work, catching up. So the house sat on, unburgled, while the smell in Joan's wardrobe turned sour.

There was no one to look after us. We needed someone

to help us go through her things: her navy Jean Muir and the Agnès B cardigans; the Biba and early Jaeger; all the stuff she bought that famous year she spent in London before my father met her and courted her and brought her back home.

Isn't that what men are for? To tell you it's only a skirt, for God's sake, it's only an old blouse. But the men left us to it, and even if they hadn't, the fact was that neither Shay nor Conor were up to the job. They didn't matter enough. They could not keep us safe from each other, as we took out her Sybil Connolly evening stole, or the little ostrich-feather shrug, and said, 'No you have it,' 'No you.'

It was more than a question of timing, is what I am saying, though timing is what we think about now.

Outside in the garden, tethered to the gate with some vicious, strong wire, the For Sale sign stands; bright and square and always new. It was hammered in there seventeen months ago, give or take. There is no point arguing about it. Anyone can do the dates. Anyone can do the sums. It is what it is – that's what I say. *It is what it is.* Our mother died in May 2007. She was dead all day. She would be dead for the rest of that week. And the week after that, she would be dead too. It was no longer, for Joan, a question of timing.

And anyway, we thought – we were in the habit of thinking – that the longer you left it, the better. Just that February, Mrs Cullen's down the road went Sale Agreed at 'nearly two'. That is how you spoke about these things that spring, during the last furious buying before all the buying stopped, when the word 'million' was too real and dirty to say out loud. Way back in the good old days, when my mother was alive, and everyone drank in the streets and, if you wanted your kitchen tiled (and we wanted little else), you had to fly the workman in from England, and put him up in a hotel.

Shay brought us to the solicitor's, sometime in early June. We sat in his office in town and let this stranger with his fine, clean hands go through a file marked 'Miles Moynihan' and opine, in the casual after-chat, that once probate was cleared we would probably ask for 'two and a bit'.

Then we paid him. A big whack of money. We paid the estate agent too. Nearly two years on, I don't like any of these people.

But at the time, I was almost grateful. If you're going to spin your grief into cash – what the hell – maybe it helps if the cash is crazy. We left his office and walked in silence down the granite steps. Fiona said, 'Nice hands.'

'He was wearing Alexander McQueen shoes,' I said. 'Did you see? Tiny little skulls in the leather.'

'What does that mean?' she said. 'What does that *mean*?'

'It means he's a filthy rich, post-punk solicitor.'

'Well that's all right then. That makes me feel a lot better.'

When I think about it now, I suspect he knew something we did not. I suspect they all did, that they just couldn't say it, not even to themselves. We spoke to an estate agent in July and there was some talk of probate, but the timing was good, he said, for the autumn market, so we put the house up for sale in the first week in September, whether we owned it or not. It went on the websites on Wednesday, it was in the property supplement on Thursday. We sat back and felt that we had managed something hugely difficult and significant. We did not want to let the place go.

We do now.

I catch my mother's trail around the kitchen, this morning of snow, and I am grateful for it. Some days, it doesn't feel like the house I grew up in, anymore. I don't remember that I own it, or even half of it. That is what I should have said to my sister when we were still shouting at each other. *I will only live in half.* Although I am not living there, as we know. I am only keeping the place in a condition to view.

Most of the small stuff is sorted now, gone to the dump or the charity shop, to Fiona's house or over to Clonskeagh. We divided it with great tenderness. *No you take it, No you.* These foolish, small pieces of cloth, that no one will ever wear again, a useful triple steamer, a few abstract oils that scream '1973'.

Every once in a while, I come across something we missed. After Seán moved in (though he never actually 'moved in') I found a photograph fallen down the back of a chest of drawers; a large glossy black-and-white picture of our parents standing in front of the control tower in Dublin airport. Going where – Nice? Cannes? Going to Lourdes, probably, with rosary beads in her patent handbag – though they managed, with her crocheted hat and his flapping trench, to make this look like a dashing thing to do.

Another time – just a couple of months ago – I spotted a brown cloth bag on top of her wardrobe. I got on a chair and took it down. There were bottles inside: I could tell by the way the glass clacked and squeaked against itself under the cotton.

When I prised open the drawstring I found an empty bottle of Tweed, a perfume I gave her myself when I was in primary school. There was also an empty bottle of Givenchy III – the original blend – and a maverick, half-full bottle of Je Reviens. I opened the Tweed and put the cold glass under my nose, trying to conjure her out of there. Joan was old-fashioned about these things; it was the last thing she put on, after her jewellery and before her coat, so the scent of perfume will always be the smell of my mother leaving; the mystery of her bending to kiss me, or straightening back up. These were the nights when Daddy was still alive, and he would squeeze himself into a tux for some 'do' in the Burlo or the Mansion House. They would go for drinks in the Shelbourne first, and dance after dinner, in the wooden centre of the carpeted floor, to Elvis covers and 'The Tennessee Waltz'.

Then they'd come home in the middle of the night, completely lashed.

My father's dress shoes were very shiny and black. Even now, I think of them as 'drinking shoes'. I saw someone on the street, once, who was so like him. Very far gone, but immaculate with it. The kind of drinker who stays upright – also decent, and frank. The kind that likes to say 'knacker' and 'culchie', who looks like he might have more, and more cogent things to say, even when he is so steaming, the power of speech has deserted him.

I had too much wine, myself, the night after she died. After the undertaker, the phone calls and arrangements, I cracked open a Loire white, and drank it at speed, and I felt two things. The first thing I felt was nothing at all. The other thing I felt was an emotion so fake and slick I wanted rid of it. It was such a lie. There he was – my father. Not in a stranger, but in me, as I sat on my own in a straight-backed chair at the kitchen table, pausing to apologise to the wine when it slopped out of the glass.

I threw the perfume bottles away; these woody, elegant scents my mother chose to complement the smell of her cigarette smoke and her occasional night on the vodka. You might think I would want to hold on to these last moving molecules, but I did not. I wanted to open the windows, bash the upholstery, and chase the smell of her death away; the butts I found in the garden ashtray floating in rainwater, the yellow tinge on the ceilings, the cloying old glamour of Je Reviens.

SEÁN CAME TO THE FUNERAL. I didn't mind. It should have been a tactless thing to do, but it wasn't. It seemed to come from some hidden rhythm in our lives; a better place. He came up in the church porch and gave me a hug. Seán looks like someone too busy to care, but then something happens and he does it all perfectly. The country manners coming out in him, maybe, or the bank manager father, who knew the line between doing something sincerely and doing it well. Seán did it well. The only public gesture between us. The only ritual act of touching: hand on my shoulder, hand to the centre of my back, a one-armed hug, his face in my hair, 'Poor you,' he said. 'Poor Gina.' And did not pause to look into my wrecked eyes, or to feed on the sorrow in my face, but went over to hug Fiona, and then walked away. The whole sequence perfectly timed and true to what we had become; old comrades in the war of love.

My eyes were fine, as it happened. My sister's also. We are, neither of us, the crying type. We are the sunglasses type. We are the kind of woman who walks out of a funeral service talking about their foundation.

'Is there a line?' I said to Fiona, indicating the underside of my chin. Said it, and meant it. And Fiona, who understood completely, said, 'Tiny bit. Just there. You're fine.'

So my make-up was, at least, properly blended, as they loaded my mother's coffin into the hearse and Seán paid his respects in the May sunshine. I looked after him as he walked away – you might even say he trotted – a busy little shortarse in a pale summer suit, his arm up for a taxi as soon as he hit the side of the road.

Then I hugged the next person.

I can't talk about Conor at the funeral. He was great. Conor *is* great, anyone could tell you that. He did everything right. Except, I suppose, for the way he checked his damn phone every five minutes.

'Don't tell me that thing is online,' I said.

'Duh!' he said. Then he looked up at me and stalled, realising where he was.

He was wearing his black suit – too tight on him, now – his only suit, the one he had been married in. Same church, same porch, a little later in the year; the fallen cherry blossom now drifted against the steps and turning brown.

HOW CAN I BE SURE

SEÁN RANG, SOME WEEKS LATER, to 'check that I was OK', I said I was really not OK, and I laughed. He said he knew a good guy if we wanted help selling the house.

'If you *are* selling the house.'

'Well, you know,' I said. I did not tell him that I was sleeping in the place, or sleeping there some days, during the afternoon. As I said, you would think the rooms might have faded, but all her things were just as she liked them. And when I came back, one day – another day, that Fiona could not manage – I put my feet up on the sofa for a moment, and woke just as dark was starting to fall.

'What's up with you?' I said.

'Nothing's up.'

'Are you in the dogbox?' I said, because that's how he used to talk about his marriage, he always used to say, 'I'm in the dogbox at home.'

'No, it's not that,' he said. But it was something.

In the old days – the good old days, when we seldom saw each other dressed – Seán did not discuss his daughter. She might crop up towards the end of the afternoon, just as he was getting ready to go. One day he said, 'Evie wants a ferret. Can you believe it?' Another time, going through his pockets for keys, he said, 'A lump of Evie's hair fell out, have you ever seen that? About the size of an old two-pence, about this wide.'

He said this sometime in the spring. I know when it was because I remember thinking, quite casually, 'We did that.' It was our kiss on New Year's Eve that did this thing to Evie's hair.

The calls he made after Joan died were different. He rang as a friend, and he talked about his daughter, the way you do.

Evie was fighting with her mother. Evie threw a pair of shoes under the wheels of a lorry because she wanted to wear high heels. Evie was so spacey, she was always late. Her schoolwork was going to pot, she couldn't concentrate for two minutes at a time. I tried to figure out if my niece, Megan, had started her periods yet. I said, 'Is she eating?'

'Eating?' he said.

'Like, food.'

'She eats,' he said, though he seemed to disapprove of the question.

'What age is she again?'

'Ten.'

'That's a bit early all right.'

I told him we thought Fiona had anorexia when she was sixteen and this interested him a lot.

'We brought her to a doctor. Have you brought Evie to a doctor?'

'For what, though?' he said. 'I mean, what would you say?'

It was a thing we started to do, whenever I was over in Terenure – twice, maybe three times in the next couple of months – I sent him a text, and he would call. I slept on the sofa another time, and we talked when I woke. The third time (it was a bit like going back on the cigarettes, actually) I rang as soon as I got in the door, and we had these dreamy, walking chats, where he led me, through this and that, to his troublesome daughter, and I moved through my mother's rooms, and touched the objects she had left behind. And I don't know if Evie was the reason or the excuse, the day he said – maybe that day, the day of the third call:

'Where are you? Are you there now? I'm just down the road.'

Which is how we ended up making love, not in my old room, but in the bedroom beside it. I opened the front door and he was there, all clear grey eyes in front of a troubled grey sky. I showed him into the house.

'Funny,' he said.

'What?'

'I thought it would be bigger.'

'It is quite big,' I said.

We went upstairs.

'Sure,' he said. 'I mean this is a very desirable sort of house.'

He glanced inside the bedrooms, checked out the en-suite, the spare room, the upstairs bathroom.

'Two and a bit?' he said.

And then he hugged me, because I was trembling. I fended him off at the door to my parents' room and at the one that led to my own childhood bed. We went to the place of least resistance. At least I think so. I think we fell through the door that felt right.

And were, of course, found out.

SEÁN HAD COME INTO THE HOUSE with some papers in his hand and he left them on the shelf in the hall where the post gets left, and a few days later Fiona discovered, among the letters there, several addressed to him, their envelopes ripped open, including one that contained – she could not help but notice – a cheque for four-hundred-and-fifty euro. She put them in her car and drove them home on the front seat beside her, and she was about to pull into his driveway and hand them in at his door when she realised that she could not do this. She thought about pushing them through the letterbox and decided against this also. She dialled my number and said, 'I can't believe you did this to me.'

'Sorry?'

'I can't believe you did this. How am I supposed to look at them now? How am I supposed to look at his wife?'

All of this from her parked car, in the lane outside his house; the boxed fury of my sister.

'How am I supposed to look at her?'

'Look at who?' I said.

And we carried on like this for a while – like married people, shouting and lying.

'I can't believe you did this to me.'

'I didn't do it to you,' I said. 'It is nothing to do with you.'

But it turned out I had done it to everybody. The whole

world was disgusted with me and worn out by my behaviour. The entire population of Dublin felt compromised, and they felt it keenly.

Fiachra, for example, 'always knew'. He knew it before I did. 'I am in love with him,' I said, sitting in the back room of Ron Blacks after too many gin and tonics. And Fiachra waited a tiny, unforgivable moment, before he said:

'I am sure you are.'

But it was the first time I had said the words out loud, and it might have been true all along but it became properly true then. True like something you have discovered. I loved him. Through all the shouting that followed, the silences, the gossip (an unbelievable amount of gossip) there was one thing I held on to, the idea, the fact, that I loved Seán Vallely and I held my head high, even as I glowed with shame. Glowed with it.

I love him.

It was something to say in the long gaps between things – because even though it felt like everything was happening, for long stretches, nothing happened. Except for being in love, which happened intensely and all the time.

I love him: dull, like a pain, when no one rang: thrilling and clarion in the arguments I had with my sister, *I love him!* And then like a punch to the stomach, the day his wife rang to say, 'Can we talk?' and I drove up there and saw her standing behind the old glass of the house in Enniskerry, before I put the car back into gear and drove away.

'Don't mind her,' said Seán. 'I know what she's doing, here. Don't mind her. You don't know what she is like.'

But I just felt sorry for her – this woman who refused the truth. I had to remind myself this was something between me and Seán, not between me and Aileen. I might have liked her or hated her in another life. It was only incidental that she was not my type.

But this was much later – months later. For a week after that first phone call, 'I can't believe you did this to me,' Fiona did nothing. I continued as usual, and Seán continued as usual, and no one spoke to anyone else as we waited for the axe to fall.

Walking around thinking, *This will end*, and *This will end* as I stacked the dishes in Clonskeagh, or turned out the bedside light. Kissing Conor, as he slept, and feeling stupid even as I leaned over him, his stone-still, dreamless head. It was all too melodramatic and silly. Maybe the axe would not fall: maybe we would continue just as before. Though I didn't like Conor so much by then; I did not like the smell of his sleeping breath.

On Saturday morning, Seán got a call from Shay, asking him to drop round to the house. He rang me afterwards, walking back down the lane.

'What did he say?'

'Not much.'

My brother-in-law had been his rueful, back-slapping self. He brought Seán into the kitchen and pushed the letters across the table saying, 'You'll be wanting that cheque.'

'Was Fiona there?'

'No.'

Fiona had taken the kids off somewhere, apparently. Seán sounded a bit shook as he said this and I could imagine the delicate way Shay phrased it: Fiona bundling the kids into the car, as though the sight of the adulterer might scar them for life.

Another fabulous silence descended. For a week, maybe more, I waited for Seán to ring, for Aileen to turn up on my doorstep, for Conor to put his head in his hands at the desk and weep. None of these things happened. One evening after work, I went to the house in Terenure and fell asleep on the sofa. In the middle of the night I got up and went upstairs, to the bed where we last made love, and I have slept there ever since.

I WOKE TO A SKY FULL OF RAIN, and I borrowed an umbrella from my dead mother to get the bus into town – the same bus I used to get as a teenager – there wasn't a cab in sight. I went upstairs to windows thick with condensation, and the smell of wet commuters: stale lives, morning soap, last night's fun. I hadn't been on a bus in years. And I liked it. I liked looking down from this childhood height, seeing the gardens all redone, with their flagstones and big planters; the window boxes along Rathgar Road and cars guarding the gravel. The passengers were changed, too; they had funky haircuts and better clothes and they were all plugged into something, texting or listening to their headphones. We were across the canal before I realised that none of them were speaking English, and I liked that too. I had the feeling that this was the magic bus, and there was no telling our final destination.

Conor rang, sporadically, all day. I did not answer. I sat with my feet up on the desk, checking out the jobs pages of the newspapers. Undervalued, overlooked: I was completely fed up with Rathlin Communications. At four in the afternoon, the calls stopped.

He had rung Fiona.

The next few days were full of shouting. Much cliché. It seemed that everything was said. I mean everything, by everybody. The whole thing felt like a single sentence; one you could imagine bellowed, hissed, scrawled in lipstick on the bathroom mirror; you could carve it into your own flesh, you could chisel it on a fucking gravestone. And not one word of it mattered. Not one stupid word.

You never.

I always.

The thing about you is.

I think they all really enjoyed it. Fiona more than anyone. My goodness, the accusations flew.

'I am glad she is dead. I am glad our mother is dead, so she doesn't have to witness this.'

And, 'Do you think he loves you? Do you think he cares about you?'

'Yes,' I said. 'I think he does, actually.'

That was all I said. I didn't tell her she could fuck off back to her muppet of a husband, who rolls on to her after his bottle of Friday-night wine, and then rolls off again. If she calls that love. Wondering has he come yet, and how much it would cost to have a horse in livery like the woman down the road. I didn't say any of this to my sister. How I saw her being broken into mediocrity and motherhood; her body broken and then her mind – or did her mind go first, it's sort of hard to disentangle

– and then for her to turn round and say Broken is Best, I didn't say how that made me furious beyond measure.

We were in the living room of the house in Terenure. It was easy to shout there. It was like being twelve again.

I said, 'You're a prig. You're a fucking prig and you always have been. This is something for me, Fiona. Do you understand? This has nothing to do with you.'

Our mother stayed dead through all of this. Amazingly. She was dead during every tantrum and silence. And she was still dead, when we woke the next day and remembered what had been said.

Because of course you are not twelve. And you regret everything. Every word you uttered. The fact that human beings learned the art of speech – you regret that too.

STOP! IN THE NAME OF LOVE

CONOR AND I SPENT A LONG EVENING in Clonskeagh not shouting, at least for the first while. He came in while I was getting some clothes out of the Sliderobe. I always hated that thing. You could specify the finish when you signed for the house. You handed over three hundred grand and, with a special smile, they handed you a little card with squares of polished wood on it. We chose 'Birch'. Hideous. Anyway, I was taking a few things out of the Sliderobe, when I heard Conor coming up the stairs, and a few moments later he appeared in the doorway. We didn't speak. He sat on the bed and watched as I took an armful of clothes and laid them in a suitcase, with the hangers still attached. Then he got up and left the room.

When I zipped up the case and came out, I found him on the sofa, going through my Pauric Sweeney shoulderbag.

'What are you doing?'

'Are you back on the pill?' he said.

'What?' I said.

'I just want to know.'

I turned and went back into the bedroom. It was all too

sad to shout about. But, after a small silence, we managed to shout about it anyway.

'I'm your fucking husband, that's who I am!'

Conor rarely loses his temper. He does it like a cartoon, with bulging muscles and popping veins. I was almost afraid of him. And I remembered something about him that I had somehow managed to forget: how exact he was in bed; how he could, in his ruthless, friendly way, destroy me between the sheets.

'Oh right. Oh that's *right.*'

Because the unsayable thing is, that just before I started sleeping with Seán – when I was just thinking about it, when I was on the brink – myself and Conor had a lot of sex. Not the slow abandon of our early days, but rooting, rummaging, sudden sex that was not supposed to be enjoyable, strictly speaking; that was not about me. If Conor could have made me pregnant then, he would have done it without thinking (there was no thinking involved in any of this), which is why, incidentally, I think he did know about Seán, somewhere deep down.

The one thing he never said to me was that he was *surprised.*

Poor, terrifying Conor. Stood there in the halogen glare with his hands clenched and his head thrust forward. I tried to move past him to get to the stairs, but he would not give way so I stood back and thumped him in the face, quite hard. I thought I would feel pain when I hit him but a kind of numbness spread from the impact, it was like hitting rubber – not just his cheek, but my hand, the whole room seemed numb. So I swung at him again, to see if that would bring the feeling back.

Something messy happened, then. The suitcase was wrenched away from my grasp and, as I looked down, I was caught by the flat of Conor's hand across my chin. There was no pain, just a jarring dislocation; my brain moving faster than my skull. When I was steady again, I saw Conor had backed away from me and was standing against the wall, rubbing his hand. It was only then that my cheek started to sting. The delay worried me. My nerves were slow. Even when the hurt happened, I couldn't be sure that it was happening to me.

And then I was sure.

It was like that moment, many hours after the plane lands, when your ears decide to open. We looked at each other as the pain spread, and we realised that we were separate human beings.

And it exhausted us.

I waited for the script to continue, for the little surge that would make me grab my case and sling him a contemptuous glance and hurry down the stairs. But it did not come. I stood there, and lifted my face, and burst into woeful tears. Conor stepped forward and pulled my head against his shoulder and I said, 'Don't touch me. I don't want you to touch me,' but I stayed there against him. My chin was starting to ache, in the bone. I wanted a cup of tea.

We talked until four in the morning. We dredged it all up. And the things Conor told me about myself that night – 'selfish' was just the start of it – it was like a slug crawling over your soul.

'Everyone is selfish,' I said. 'They just call it something else.'

'You think?'

'I know.'

'Well you know wrong,' he said. 'Everyone is not selfish.'

I got him to bed before morning and I lay down alongside him, fully dressed. When he was asleep, I stood up, leaving the shape of myself on the duvet, and I walked out of the room. I took my bag, and the suitcase of clothes, and I took the thing he wanted most – a little boy, maybe, as yet unmade; a sturdy little runaround fella, for sitting on his shoulders, and video games down the arcade, and football in the park.

Then I went back to Terenure and texted Seán.

'Have clothes. All safe.'

Seán – who likes to use a johnny *anyway*.

Apart from anything else, how were we supposed to pay for it? The mortgage was two and a half grand a month, the childcare would be another grand on top of that. A new house – because you can't rear children in a lopsided box – would be hundreds upon hundreds of thousands more. So it didn't matter what Conor wanted, or what I wanted – I mean, I like children. I have the reproductive pang – but for all his talk of bliss betrayed, Conor was actually, when it came down to it, a dreamer.

He could do the sums as often as he liked, there was something about us as a couple that meant money made no sense to us: it was always a terrible surprise.

I don't know why.

But I am being hard on my husband, who I loved, and who is now fighting with me about money, never mind broken dreams. In fact everyone is fighting with me about money: my sister, too. Who would have thought love could be so expensive? I should sit down and calculate it out at so much per kiss. The price of this house plus the price of that house, divided by two, plus the price of the house we are in. Thousands. Every time I touch him. Hundreds of thousands. Because we took it too far. We should have stuck to car parks and hotel bedrooms (no, really, we should really have stuck to car parks and hotel bedrooms). If we keep going the price will come down – per event, as it were. Twenty years of love can be consummated for tuppence. After a lifetime it is almost free.

MONEY (THAT'S WHAT I WANT)

OUTSIDE IN THE SNOW, the For Sale sign looks fresh as the day it was hammered home. No one knows what the house is worth now. No one will buy it, so that's how much it is worth. Nothing. Despite which, we will owe tax based on that 'two and a bit'. For a house that is currently worth whistling for. I can't figure out the fake money from the real. I walk around this magic box, this trap, with its frost-flowered windows, weeping condensation as the morning proceeds. I gather my briefcase from the console table in the hall. I open the same door I have opened since I could reach the latch. And I head out to earn some money.

By the time I get to the motorway, all is quiet: a few yellow registrations, speeding back up to the border, trying to beat the weather. It's not my favourite road in Ireland – too straight and flat – though I like the epic way the clouds always seem to lower over the Mourne Mountains, the gateway to the Black North. By the time they come into view, their dark slopes are streaked with white and my phone is jumping with warnings and dire predictions. The snow is above us. It is about to fall.

'Book a hotel,' says the office. 'And stay put!'

I bailed out of Rathlin before it hit the buffers and started in the drinks industry. I wanted a new life, but it is possible I sensed what was happening, too – that autumn with my mother's house suspended, like a dream, at 'two and a bit', it is possible I sensed there was nothing under our feet.

Not that I admitted it, at the time.

Selling the house was still the answer to everything. We brought the price down from 'two and a bit' to 'nearly two' and it was still short odds on winning the lottery; it was five-hundred-and-seventy-five-thousand lamb chops, it was one-and-a-half-thousand years of lamb on your plate, it was so many shirts you would never have to wash another shirt, it was half of the townhouse in Clonskeagh and enough left over for a roof over our head, it was freedom and time to kiss, which is also called love.

But no one bought it.

Funny that.

Meanwhile I started in the drinks industry. I suspect my family thought the Sheilses a bit vulgar for being publicans but, you know, Conor's father might have been low enough to sell the stuff, but my father was low enough to drink it. Maybe, in my separated, orphaned state, I realised what side I was finally on. Good times or bad, I thought, there will always be Al Co Hol.

As it turned out, the bad times were already upon us and what started out as a new and exciting web-based viral marketing campaign turned into me in a VW Golf, putting girls in bikinis into bars with trays of flavoured vodka. Which is about as far away from the future of the world wide web as you can get. It sure sells vodka though, and there is very little I don't know, now, about fake tan. I'm like this really drawly air hostess I heard over the intercom once, then realised it was the captain speaking, and she wasn't offering us drinks and snacks. 'Em, yeah, nothing much to report here, folks, we're cruising now at twenty-thousand feet, bit of a tailwind . . .' So I'm the really drawly one, in this bevy of bottle blondes with goosebumps on their Xen Tan Absolute. I am all white, and all real, I keep my clothes on and earn many times what they do, despite which I am pushed, sometimes actually shoved aside by local press, publicans, and many hundreds of drunken men, every second Friday night, from 5.30 to 9 p.m. Some of the men pause to sneer at me first, or they turn to sneer at me after, *Yeah, look what we got.* There is an amount of what you might call collateral anger to mop up. And there's always one guy – a nice guy, a good guy – who decides, in all the excitement, that the girl to hit on is the one wearing the clothes. For this, I get paid. I'm a pimp. It's a funny life.

But I am not going up to Dundalk to do a promotion, I am going up to Dundalk to let two of the sales staff go, after which, one of them will be taken back at a casual rate. I'm still relatively new, so I am the one who gets to fire people, the unspoken suggestion being, of course, that the last person I fire may be myself.

The office is a couple of rooms tacked on to a warehouse near the M1: grey walls, grey roof, blue carpet, red banisters, yellow cubes to set your coffee cup down. It is hard to think that people work here. No voices are ever raised. Nothing feels used.

I set up in the small meeting room and call the girls in, one at a time. I keep it neat and light, because that's the way I like to work, but I can't help but be caught by the look in their eyes. I am not saying I enjoy it, but you spend your time pretending you're not actually the boss, that you're all just friends, and they still bitch about you like crazy. Now the pretending was over. With benefits and casual hours they wouldn't do too badly, but still you could feel it, the first snappings, strand by strand, as the rope started to go: Sinéad, with four-hundred-and-twenty points in her Leaving Certificate and a mouthful of veneers she got on the HP. Alice, who was a hippy chick at heart, just saving up for her trip to Peru. I said I would fight for the best possible package. I told them that human resources would be in touch. Then I stood up and offered my hand to shake. Then a hug, because we were all just friends really. And then they left. I did some photocopying, put my head around the distribution manager's door – he was already heading home – then I walked out through the warehouse floor. I ducked under gallons of hooch raised in a toast on an abandoned fork-lift – there it all was: drink stacked high, walls of drink, drink on the move.

I drove back to the interchange and, after five miles of road, the car was swallowed by the soft and oncoming storm; a dream of red tail lights, in a dirty white mess of snow. Everything was so quiet, and the other drivers so gentle; I should have been worried, but there was something about this slow danger that was comforting and lovely. I don't know how long it lasted. By the time I passed the airport, the air was clear. Seán was in there somewhere, in a welter of cancellations. The passengers were running from gate to gate, 'like a herd of bullocks,' he said. I crouched over the steering wheel and looked up, but the sky I saw through the windscreen was already dark and empty of planes.

It was half past four.

According to the radio, the entire country had bailed out of work early and was heading for home. I expected Dublin to be bedlam, but the port tunnel was so empty and pure it felt like the future, and the quays, when I surfaced in the dark of the city centre, were deserted. I imagined the traffic spreading like an aftershock, washing up in a dirty rim in the foothills of the Dublin mountains, where the pure snow began.

The schools had closed early. I wondered about Evie, if her mum would get there to pick her up, or how she would manage. I went to dial her number and then I didn't. I have never actually rung Evie, though we are perfectly happy to talk if, by some accident, we end up on the phone.

BACK IN TERENURE the house was dark and empty and cold. I turned on the heat and checked my emails, but I found it hard to settle. I was waiting for Seán to come home but he had not even left yet. It made me strangely angry, the thought of him sitting at the seafood bar, with a plate of smoked salmon and a glass of white. Neither here nor there. A man not unaccustomed to the departure lounge.

It took Seán seven months to leave Enniskerry. For seven

months, after I left Conor, he got out of my bed and got in his car and drove home, so he could be there in the morning to make his daughter's porridge (with cinnamon) and kiss her mother goodbye.

Just a peck, of course.

Seven months, I wasn't allowed to ring or text or email, because it was more important than ever to be secret now; our love more urgent and sweet in these last days before he went clear.

But he did not go clear. After Christmas, he said. He could not do it before Christmas. They were buying Evie her first laptop; a little netbook. He wanted one himself, if only he could afford it, he said. And he laughed.

That Christmas – I can not even think about that Christmas. Whoever invented Christmas should be shot.

And when he finally washed up on my doorstep at two in the morning, after who knows what storm; when he finally broke free of her that spring and came to me, he did not come to live, but just to escape. He still spends the occasional night out – I assume in Enniskerry. I do not ask. In Ireland, if you leave the house and there is a divorce, then you will lose the house, he says. You have to sleep there to keep your claim. Which was all news to me, but there you go. You think it is about sex, and then you remember the money.

So here we are, some nights: me sleeping in my sister's bed in Terenure. Seán sleeping in the au pair's room in Enniskerry, where we kissed, or perhaps even in his old bedroom, beside the aggrieved body of his wife. Seán somewhere asleep, between the ageing flesh of his wife and the growing flesh of his child. Who knows where is he sleeping, in his dreams?

'I never remember my dreams,' he says.

It is not just the snow that makes me wonder these things. Though it is also, perhaps, the snow. It is Seán's voice on the phone finally landed in Budapest, sounding just like himself and so far away.

'Fucking Ryanair,' he says.

'Well, yes.'

'We were sitting on the tarmac for an hour and a half, I looked out the window and there was a man at the wing with a shovel. He was taking the ice off with an actual shovel, and there was a kind of rope with two men hanging on to it, jumping up and down. They were sawing back and forth, with this rope thrown over the wings. Which was bad enough. I mean sitting there watching it was bad enough. But then we took off.'

'Jesus. Were there lights?'

'What do you mean, lights?'

'I don't know. Snow lights. Or something.'

I need to see him safe in his plane. I need to look in through the porthole windows, with blue lights and white lights flashing in the darkness, like a fifties movie set; the snow swirling outside. And, as if he has guessed my problem, Seán says, 'The man was not standing on the wing. Believe me, I checked.'

'How's Budapest? Is it snowing there?'

'No actually,' he says. 'Listen, Gina.'

I know if he says my name, he wants to talk about Evie. Or

not talk about Evie, he wants to tell me of some arrangement involving Evie that I will not have the power to change.

'What?'

'Everything's had to be pushed forward. I don't know if I can get back tomorrow afternoon.'

'When can you get back?'

'I don't know. Definitely Saturday. If it doesn't snow.'

'Tell me when you know, will you?'

'Of course.'

'How's Budapest?'

'Is that where I am?'

He sounds worn out. I can hear the news on his hotel TV.

'Have yourself a nice bath,' I say.

'I don't do baths.'

'No?'

'Not in hotels. You don't know who's been there before you.'

It takes me a while to hear this, or to make sense of it. I am listening to the space he occupies, I am listening to his breath, to the timbre of his voice, that is the same to me, almost, as the texture of his skin. It has the same effect. Or better. I am closer listening to him than touching him.

'Sure give it a wipe,' I say.

I could live on the phone.

Evie, it turns out, has – I actually blank this bit of the conversation out. Seán says, 'On Saturday morning, Evie has . . .' and my brain goes 'tweet tweet, oh is that the time, how pretty' and I look out at the garden and beyond to the traffic lights, casting their beautiful light, as they switch senselessly from red to green across the serene stretch of tyre-mangled snow. So, Evie has, I don't know; horse riding or a play date or drama or the orthodontist, which means that – tweet tweet – Seán will have to pick her up on Friday from the city centre, or Enniskerry, or outside her school if there is school, except it will not be Seán because he is not here, and I say, 'Fine, no problem,' realising after I have put the phone down that Seán is saying something new here. He is saying that because of circumstances that have released a whole flock of sparrows in my brain, I may have to pick up Evie tomorrow. I myself will have to do it, while Seán, presumably, flies home.

Great.

Aileen, of course, must not be disturbed on this one. Aileen must not be humiliated further. It would never be possible for Aileen to ring the bell of my home, or to meet me in the street in order to hand her child to me. Her child. To me. That would not be possible. That would be like dying. And no one wants Aileen to die in this particular way.

I will never be rid of that woman.

The first few months together in Terenure, everything reminded Seán of how much he hated Aileen. Especially me. Everything I did reminded him of his wife.

One morning, I told him he would catch a cold. This was in the early days, after the bike was bought but before he had figured the clothes, so he went out in his shirtsleeves, folding his suit jacket over the handlebars.

'Careful you don't catch cold,' I said, watching from the front door, and he went still for a moment before getting up on the bike and cycling away.

That evening we fought about something stupid – our first

domestic – and it turned out, once the spat was over, that I had reminded him of his wife. Because whenever Seán was going on a plane, in whatever season, autumn or spring – he could never remember what way it went – travelling to a warmer country or a colder one, Aileen would always say, 'You'll get a cold, you know,' and she was always, but always, right. And Seán hated it. It was like she owned his entire immune system. And anyway, what was he supposed to do, stay at home?

There was a wasted intensity in the way he spoke about her; nailing the lid down on some coffin with nothing inside it. Or, what was inside? A joke. Some zombie wife who still twitched at the light. I spent my days trying to guess what Aileen might say, so I could say something different – and I learned, in jig time, not to mention illness of any kind. Or weakness even. I learned not to make him feel weak in any way.

I don't know what she did to him, but she sure did it good.

It was a delicate business, being the Not Wife. That morning he looked at the clean shirt he took out of the wardrobe and said, 'Is there something wrong with the iron?' Both of us stopping right there. It was not that Aileen did Seán's shirts. Aileen had a Polish girl in to do Seán's shirts at twelve euro an hour. But if Seán was going to live like a younger man, he would have to change.

And he did change.

A second intimacy can be very sweet. There are so many mistakes you do not have to make. I could not believe he was beside me when I fell asleep. I could not believe he was beside me when I woke. We went to the supermarket; picking up boxes of laundry tablets like Bonnie and Clyde.

'What about these ones? You think?'

Our shoes leaving bloody footprints, all the way down the aisle.

We did the things that boring couples do: Seán cooked dinner sometimes, and I lit the candles. We went to the pictures, and for that weekend to Budapest. We even went for walks – out into the world, side by side. Seán held my hand. He was proud of me. He took an interest in my clothes and told me what to wear. He wanted me to look good. He wanted me to look good for waiters and other strangers, because we still didn't meet his friends. Which suited me fine, I couldn't take the pressure.

We were out one night in Fallon & Byrne's when a woman stopped by the table.

'My goodness,' she said. 'Would you look who it is.'

I did not recognise her.

'That's right,' said Seán.

'So look at you.'

She was drunk. And middle-aged. It was the Global Tax woman, the one who was there at the conference in Montreux. She chatted for a minute and then sidled back to her own table, giving me a twee, ironic little wave before sitting in with her friends.

'Don't mind her,' said Seán.

'I don't.' I went back to my dinner. I said, 'She just looks so old.'

Seán looked at me, as though from a new and lonely distance.

'She didn't always,' he said.

'When was it, anyway?'

'It was . . . a long time ago.'

Later, as though to remind me that it comes to us all, he said, 'She was the same age as you are now, actually.'

And he pulled my lip with his teeth, when he kissed me.

No wonder she shrieked and writhed, the zombie wife. I thought – just in flashes – that I was actually turning into her.

I had to trust him, he said. Our second row, this, when I expected him home and he did not arrive till late – I had to trust him because he had given up everything for me. Because Aileen had doubted every word that came out of his mouth. He could not live with that again. There were times he thought she needed to be jealous: that jealousy was part of her sexual machine.

Believe me, I thought about that one for a while.

Meanwhile, we never had any tomato chutney and the cheese I bought was just bizarre.

'Come to bed.'

'In a minute.'

'Come to bed.'

'I said, "in a minute".'

'You said that a minute ago.'

Seán told me that I have saved his life.

'You saved my life,' he said. And every small thing about me is wrong. I eat too much, I laugh the wrong way. I am not allowed to order lobster off a menu; the sight of me sucking out the meat would, he said, last him a very long time. He holds me by the hips, and squeezes, testing for fat. If it hadn't been for me, he says, *If it hadn't been for you* and he kisses me, on the side of the neck, lifting my hair.

I have saved his life.

My mother is still dead.

The snow does not accuse, or not particularly. But I am alone and I do not know for how long. There is nothing on the internet. The TV rattles on. I sacked two people today, in Dundalk. I mean, I had to let them go. I sit at my laptop with my phone in my hand and wonder how the hell I got here. And where it all went wrong. If it did go wrong. Which it did not, of course. Nothing, as I am tired of saying, went wrong.

What was the last thing he said from Budapest?

'Goodnight, Gorgeous.'

'Goodnight.'

'Goodnight, my love,' whispering ourselves off the line.

'Night night.'

Trailing our talk down to the fingertips.

'Night.'

And gone.

SAVE THE LAST DANCE FOR ME

THOSE FIRST MONTHS IN TERENURE, Seán did not talk about Evie, or mention her much, and I was so stupid, I did not realise he could not bring himself to say her name.

No one came to visit. It was strange, because this has always been an open kind of house – my mother used to complain about it, the way people would drop in almost unannounced. But no one dropped in on the fornicators, the love-birds and home-wreckers in No. 4. The phone stayed mute: we did not even rent the line.

I said it to Fiachra: 'We're pariahs,' and, as if to prove me wrong, he rocked up one Saturday morning with a bag of croissants, and a baby buggy the size of a small car.

It took all three of us to get it through the porch and parked in the hall. In the middle of this operation, Fiachra, who is a lanky object, bent over his daughter and unclipped the straps. He lifted her out and handed her to Seán, who without even a feint of surprise, set her on his hip, using his free hand to manipulate the thing closer to the wall. The child started to reach for her father just as Seán started to hand her back to him, and it was all quite deftly done. But Seán followed her with his face and, at the last moment, nuzzled into her fine, blonde hair.

Then he followed her head a little further. And inhaled.

It was unnatural. They might as well have been kissing, my lover and my friend, each of them attached to this large construction of wriggle and big blue eyes and spit.

But Seán wasn't looking into her eyes. He was smelling her head. His own eyes were closed.

Fiachra said, 'Watch out, she is a stranger to soap,' and Seán gave a tiny grunt of appreciation.

'Who's a great girl?' he said, pulling back to look at her. He jiggled her foot, which dangled from the crook of Fiachra's arm. 'Who's a great girl?'

I am not saying it was sexual, I am saying it was a moment of great physical intimacy, and that it took place in my mother's hall while I held a bag of warm croissants and looked on.

'Coffee?' I said.

'Lovely.'

'Yes, please.'

But no one moved.

After this first frankness, Seán appeared to ignore the child, who was, I have to say, a sweetie. She sat on her father's lap and ate her croissant with close and reverential attention while Fiachra told stories about his new life as a stay-at-home Dad. He was queuing up in Cumberland Street dole office with the junkies, he said, his round-eyed daughter watching from her Hummer-buggy, when the guy in front of him holds up a little white plastic newsagent's knife and waves it around saying, 'I'll cut myself, I'll fuckin' cut myself!' The cop snapping on latex gloves as he moves, big and easy, across the floor.

'God almighty.'

Seán leaned against the counter, and laughed. He moved to set the coffee pot further back on the stove. He went over to the bin and tucked the plastic bin-liner into place. He walked out to the hall, as though there was someone at the door, and then came back in again. After a while I realised that he wasn't so much ignoring the child as prowling around it. He approached and avoided her, all the time. He was like something on David Attenborough, I told him later, one of those silverback gorillas maybe, who has forgotten where baby gorillas come from, then Mammy Gorilla pops one out, and he doesn't know what to do. Cuddle it? Eat it? Pick it up and throw it in a bush?

'Are you finished?' he said.

'Probably,' I said.

'Good,' he said. Then he walked out of the kitchen and did not come back for three days.

I had been so stupid. It wasn't about Aileen – this anguish I had to live with, and avoid, and constantly tend. It was about Evie.

'I failed her,' he said.

He stood at the counter with the window at his back, the same place and silhouette as when he watched Fiachra's child cover herself in apricot jam. It was July, and nothing was figured out yet, not even a holiday. Seán rubbed his hands up over his face, then scrubbed his scalp at the bottom of his skull. His mouth and chin distorted and his eyes shut tight. His throat produced a kind of whine, and tears popped from between his eyelids, round and clear.

He wept. And this was clearly something he had very little practice doing. Seán, the charmer, could not cry in a charming way. He cried like a mutant, all twisted and ingrown.

It did not last long. I made him a Bloody Mary and he sat at the table to drink it. He would not be hugged or touched – I did not try. How could he have done it, he said. To fail a child, it was beyond comprehending. It was not possible to fail a child. But he had done it. He had done the impossible thing.

I held him later, in the darkness, and told him the whole project is about failure. It has failure built in.

AT THE END OF AUGUST, Seán brought me with him to Budapest to make up for the way my summer had been laid waste by loving a family man. We walked along the Danube and talked about what he was going to do, and he started to tell me about Evie.

When she was four, he said, Evie fell off a swing in the back garden in Enniskerry and they thought she had concussion. The au pair did not even see it happen, she just looked around to find the child gone, and the plastic seat of the swing still moving. Aileen arrived home to find Evie unwakeably asleep at half six in the evening. There was a trickle of dried blood coming down from the child's mouth – not much – where she had bitten the inside of her cheek and her pants had been soiled.

'I change her,' said the au pair. And she shrugged, as though she was expected to live among savages.

When Seán walked in sometime later, he found his wife

trembling in an armchair, Evie watching the 'Teletubbies' with a wan, important look on her face and the au pair upstairs, talking a mile a minute into the landline – presumably to her parents – in Spanish. Aileen had, in fact, slapped the girl but Seán was not to know this for some time: it was something he would discover later, when the arguments began. And though the room upstairs was always called the au pair's room, this was despite the fact that there was no actual au pair after this, and from then on – from that moment on – his life was just.

'What?'

'Unexpected,' he said.

And we turned from the river wall, where he had been watching the water below, and we walked on.

Apart from some speeding cyclists, the quays were quiet. We went across an iron bridge that was guarded by four beautiful iron birds. I said, 'Bring her to Terenure.'

'I can't,' he said.

'Why not?'

'I just can't.'

'Some Friday when I am away. Try it. Just bring her through the door.'

WHEN WE GOT BACK to Terenure, he looked around with an assessing eye. Then he went to the pink shop and bought her a pink duvet and a pink pillow. He also bought a matching net princess canopy for over the bed.

'I couldn't pass it,' he said.

I said, 'What age is she again?'

So he went back into town and swapped the pink bed linen

for some with a chopped fruit design in acid-yellow and lime-green. He bought a lime-coloured dressing gown with purple trim, and oversized slippers with doggy faces on the toes.

He bought an iPod dock in the shape of a plastic pig and a little white chest of drawers to put it on. He bought a fish bowl and a goldfish, in a clear plastic bag. I said, 'Who is going to feed the fish?'

'I will,' he said.

He gave it to me for a moment, and I held it up to the light. An orange fish, darting and stopping in its bright bubble of water.

Happiness in a bag.

Seán fed it for at least a month, every second day, faithfully, then one evening, I got a text: 'check fish!!!!!!!!!!!'

So I feed it now, and it is still alive. A fish called Scratch. You can hear it when the house is still – actually hear it – nose down, picking up stones, sorting through the gravel. The first time she stayed over, Evie said the sound of it kept her awake all night, it was the noisiest fish on the planet.

EVEN SCRATCH IS QUIET, tonight. It has started to snow again and the tyre-welts on the street are softening into humps and mounds of white. The traffic lights work on. Upstairs, at the end of the landing, Evie's room is a padded shrine of lime-green and acid-yellow, with pips, in the watermelon smiles of blood red. Her clothes, in the little white chest of drawers, tend more to black as the months pass, with rips in the right places, and skulls, and scrag-ends of tulle. Her father lets her wear what she likes. He talked about a carpet, so her sequinned hi-tops would have something to look good on, while she is away. It is like he has forgotten where he is.

'A *new* carpet?' I said.

'Maybe a rug.'

So I hoover the rug.

I did not pay for the rug.

I nearly paid for it, mind you – that woman is bleeding him dry.

The rug has big coloured squares on it. It looks great. And I am not complaining. When it comes to housework, Seán is a clean sort. You don't catch him at it, but after he has been through, the place is brighter, neater. His laundry tablets may glow in the dark, but they make my clothes smell like sunshine itself.

He is asleep now, wherever he is. He is dreaming figures, calculations, presentations: he is dreaming about rooms. There are women in those rooms, but do not ask him, when he wakes, which women they are.

'I never dream about people I know. Rarely,' he says.

I close the lid of my laptop and listen. There is a sound in the house – a sound like the fish, but it is not the fish. Something tiny.

I go through the rooms downstairs, but the noise seems to move about as I try to follow it. I pull up cushions from the sofa, and listen at the chimney breast. I go out and head up the stairs, only to pause before I reach the landing. It is somewhere between the top of the stairs and the bottom of the stairs. I go up and then down. I turn and turn about. I stand still and listen.

Finally, in a rush, I pull Seán's gym bag out from the cupboard under the stairs. His kit is in the wash, but his trainers are still in there, also a toilet bag, and a loose tin of talc. I drag on some neon-green wires until the headset of his iPod comes into view. It is one of those jogging headsets, with a stiff band that rests on the back of your neck; the kind that looks a bit stupid even if you are actually jogging. It takes me a moment to pull the thing free. The music seems so small and frantic, locked up in there. I put one of the buds to my ear, the band twisting against my cheek, and I hear it open up, a whole cathedral of sound.

'Listen to this,' he said one night. 'Listen to this!' slotting the iPod into Evie's plastic-pig speaker dock; some smiling diva on the display, and a voice – once you got over the swoop and posh of it – singing something no one should be asked to understand.

There she is again, dangling at the other end of the luminous wire. The 'Four Last Songs' with Elizabeth Schwarzkopf. Surely he wasn't pounding the treadmill to the 'Four Last Songs'? I sit on the floor and listen for another while, before switching the thing off and throwing it back into the staleness of the gym bag. I do not linger. I do not unzip the side pockets, or check his toiletries, or lift the rectangular base of the bag to see if there is a condom under there, long forgotten, or freshly stashed. I just pause the iPod and push the lot back under the stairs.

That is how quiet Dublin is, on this night of snow.

My father listening to classical music in the dining room; his papers in piles on the polished table, the sunset making the room thick with colour. The beauty of it.

Don't annoy your father now.

My father sitting in the chair, eyes closed, one arm hanging by his side; dead, or asleep. Passionately dead. Passionately asleep. Or maybe he was just out of it. What was the music?

Ravel's *Boléro*.

Ah. The nineteen-eighties.

I get to my feet and he is behind me as I turn, talking into the phone, smoking into the old-fashioned cold of the hall. He spent his life out here, conducting cheery conversations about nothing you could put a finger on. We used to listen, myself and Fiona, to see if he would say something we could understand; a word like 'money' or 'intestate' or even 'county council', but he could go twenty minutes straight without nouns, or names, or anything you could stick a meaning to. 'That's the way of it,' he said, or, 'Well, he would, wouldn't he,' along with much chortling of a professional nature. All the time playing some deliberate game with the lighted cigarette that was in his hand, laying it with precision at the edge of the table, then nosing it along, to keep the burning tip ahead of the wood.

'Indeed, you might say that. Ha ha. You might.'

And later, in the dining room, when the music could not hold him, I remember our father getting agitated at the dusk, turning to the window over and over as if to ask, What is happening to the light? Like a dog during a solar eclipse, my mother said. This was in his last illness. He had some funny bile thing that affected his liver and the toxins in his blood caused a quick kind of havoc in his brain. The world refused to make sense to him, even as it turned. It took us a while to notice – dementia gave my father a bluff and paranoid air. He became more hearty, and trusted no one. It was *just as he had always suspected.*

One afternoon I came back from the swimming pool in Terenure College with my hair wet. There must have been boys there; something about me that looked like guilt.

'Why is that one wet?' he said, and he looked to Fiona, like I was the greatest eejit.

'She went for a swim, Daddy.'

'A swim?'

It was hard to know what part of the sentence he did not understand; whether he had forgotten about swimming, or forgotten about water, or forgotten, indeed, about wetness. But he did not forget, not to the very end, how to pitch one human being against the other. That he could do when all else was lost to him.

'A woman should be very beautiful or very interesting,' he used to say, when he was well. 'And you, my dear, are *madly* interesting.'

Pronounced 'medley', in that lush, Irish camp he liked to affect when he delivered his bon mots. Fiona, of course, was *medley* beautiful.

Neither did he forget how to drink. Fiona would dispute this, but I have the clearest memory of us both walking down to the hospice on Harold's Cross Road with a naggin of gin that we had bought for him in the off-licence before the park. We had saved our pocket money for it.

He was sitting up in the bed when we found his room, but he did not know who we were. He said to Fiona, 'Who are you? Why are you kissing me?' But he still remembered the difference between vodka and gin – it was supposed to look like water, we knew that much, but it seems we got the wrong one – he spat it back into the tooth mug, and said, 'What do you call this?'

Then he drank it anyway.

It was as though he was made of glass, his insides had gone so slack and loud. You could hear the liquid travelling into his stomach, spilling down his oesophagus, gurgling into his belly. There was a wrung-out kind of creak as it rose back up and the expression on his face as he willed it down again was comically fierce. He closed his eyes and rested. Then he opened them again and, for two minutes, maybe five, he was completely himself. He was the man we knew; clever, busy, large.

'If you stopped biting your lips, my dear, then you wouldn't have such a raggedy mouth.'

My father used to complain about my mouth, the way it gave me an insolent look. 'What's the puss about?' he said, or once, memorably, to one of his cronies, 'She didn't get that, sucking oranges through a tennis racket.'

But he said plenty of nice things, too. My father never treated us as children. If you hurt him, he would hurt you right back. If you made him laugh, he would bring the house down with delight. I don't remember people 'doing' children, the way Fiona 'does' hers in that *tidy your toys and we'll have a nice hug* sort of way. There was drama all day when my father was around, and it was all as big as it needed to be. He fought with my mother, he loved my mother. He went missing. He came home and was shaggy and large with us. I loved that about him, the wonderful air of danger and surprise.

I just hated, as I got older, the look of him when he had drink taken: the way he swivelled his face around to find you, and the chosen, careful nonsense that came out of his mouth when he did. I hated the way he sat there, benignly absent, or horribly possessed by some slow creature, who rolled, across the distance between you, whatever sentence he could shape in his head; lovely, mean, grandiose, small. Or fond: that was the worst, I think. Fond.

'Look at you. Aren't you lovely?'

By the time we were teenagers, he wasn't around all that much. He always kept Sunday at home, but even on a Sunday he was in bed till eleven, and went out around five so, let's face it, six hours a week, a bit of roast lamb with mint sauce on the side – you could take it either way. You could be mad about him, as Fiona was, you could be pretty and perfect, you could have plaits that were sweet, and hairbands that stayed put, you could work on your Irish dancing and your songs from *Oklahoma!* or you could slob about and glower, like me. I was clever. I mean, Fiona was clever in a let's-all-get-a-B-plus sort of way, but I was clever because if I was clever then I would not have to care.

Now she has a perfect life, my sister has taken to inventing a perfect past to match it. She doesn't think our father was a drunk – which makes two of them, I suppose – and she would certainly deny the memory I have of us hanging on to each other laughing, coming back up the Harold's Cross Road.

'Who are you? Why are you kissing me?' he had said to her. 'And why, my pet, have you stopped kissing me, when we were getting so nicely acquainted?'

Demented is different to drunk. I think people get demented the same way they get annoying. The thing you don't like about them just gets worse, until one day you find that's all there is left of them – the fuss and the show of it – the actual person has snuck out the back and gone home.

I can't remember how long his illness took. Too long. Not long enough. When the school holidays came, we were sent across to our Granny O'Dea's house in Sutton where the sea lapped the garden steps or exposed a rocky shore and sometime, between one tide and the next, he died.

At the funeral, then, we got him back: this wonderful person, our father. The church was packed, the house overflowed with men in suits, who sat and leaned their hands on long thighs, to tell tales of his wit, his acumen, his canny charm. He was the last of the great romantics. My mother said that. Someone had sent a case of Moët, and she asked for it to be served. She stood up and raised her glass. She said, 'Here's to Miles, my handsome husband. He was the last of the great romantics.'

Why not?

Then they left and we were alone.

We had a way, all that autumn, of hanging out and moping – that's the only way to describe it: the three of us talking about clothes and hair and weight, pecking at things, idling them through our fingers, going on the same diets, swapping clothes; stealing from each other too.

'Did you take my halterneck top?'

'What top?'

And nothing in these conversations was ever satisfactory,

or wanted to be, there was only one direction, and that was downhill.

When Fiona hit seven stone my mother brought her to a shrink, who said my sister had stopped eating in order to stop the clock: if she stayed a child, then her father would not have to die. Which was too sad to be useful really. Joan went back to wearing her dressing gown all day and Fiona went back to her cottage cheese and there was no food in the fridge anyway – at least not after I had been through it – and then, when the spring came, we discovered boys.

Or I discovered boys. Fiona, if you ask me, only pretended to.

People might think it hard, growing up with a pretty sister but Fiona was lovely the way girls are lovely for their Daddy, and after he died, she did not know what to do with it, really. Her beauty was a sort of puzzle to her. And she always ended up with the wrong sort of guy: the kind who want a girlfriend to match their car; prestige types, bottom feeders, liars. At least that's what I think; that boring old Shay was probably the best of them. That she ran into motherhood in the hopes that she would be safe there, and they would all leave her alone.

But in the spring of 1989, six months after Miles died, my sister was pretty and I was lots of fun. Joan screwed a fag into her white plastic filter, and got out the powder and blush. We were the Moynihans of Terenure. It was our duty to have a queue of young men knocking at the door.

ACROSS THE ROAD – which is now a busy road – is the bus stop where I used to say goodnight to those early boyfriends:

sitting on the wall for hours, or strolling around the corner on some excuse ('Let's see what's around the corner!'), for a bout of kissing. Rory or Davey or Colin or Fergus: it was supposed to be about their eyes or their fringe or their taste in music, but despite the way I persuaded myself, with doodles in the backs of copy books and shrieks among friends, that I loved them, each in turn, it was all just about this: the smell of petrol from the buses, and the evenings getting longer, and kissing outdoors until the tips of our noses went cold. In those days, just being in the open air gave me goosebumps. Walking down the street alone, thinking my beautiful thoughts, picking the yellow blooms off the neighbour's forsythia and shredding them on to the path: kissing was the answer to all this too.

It took me a long time to move on to anything more serious, sexually: Fiona too, I think. The Moynihan girls were old-fashioned. It was something to do with our mother being a widow; an instinct we had about power.

It was Fiona I missed, that first Christmas back in Terenure. Seán was in Enniskerry doing Santa Claus for a child who no longer believed in Santa Claus. Aileen was serving a light fino before lunch. I was alone. And the person I missed was my sister, the woman who was glad – as she said, *glad* – our mother was dead, so she wouldn't have to witness the way I was carrying on.

She was wrong about that, by the way. My mother would have understood. My mother with her handsome, infuriating husband; she would have kissed the top of my sad head.

I slip between the curtains in the front room and press my

forehead to the glass, with the nets falling down my back, the orange light of the streetlights outside turning the shadows violet, and I remember, or think I remember, some childhood snow, Miles bringing us to the big hill in Bushy Park, half the neighbourhood going down it on tea trays and body boards and plastic bags, Hold on tight! The outraged ducks slipping across the obstinate pond, our screams bouncing off a low, blank sky.

Miles in the room behind me, with the rug rolled up, old twinkle toes.

Once round the dresser!

Teaching me Irish dancing, singing out the patter: one two three, one two three, *down*-kick and tip and heel-*fall*, bang, kick up, heel-step tip-drum.

And just for a moment, I do not care what kind of a man he was. Perhaps it is the way the snow opens up a space, but for a moment, all my memories of my father are chocolate-box, and smell of winter: icing sugar thrown on the fire, in a shower of yellow flame, a crate of satsumas cold from the garage, my mother in a Nordic knit, Miles with a daughter under each arm standing on the doorstep, listening to Mr Thomson down the road, playing 'Silent Night' on his military bugle. Of course Christmas in this house was always a bit of a torment – there was always, before the day was out, some crisis with handsome, pissed old Miles – but it started well. Bursting through the door to find our presents in heaps at either end of the sofa – Fiona's one end, mine the other – a big comfortable sofa, the fabric a dark embossed red; picked out, along the seams, with a beige fringe.

THERE I AM, on my father's knee, a little pietà. I am waiting to be tickled, playing dead.

My father lifts one hand and holds it high.

'Is that the way?'

'I'm dead!'

I start to wriggle to the floor and, as I slip across his knees, he pounces, finding the spaces between my ribs and digging in. By the time I have hit the carpet I am beside myself. I am out of my skin, stuck to the spinning floor. I am tied to my body where his fingers hold me together, as I fly apart.

'No! No!'

My father tickling me from the sofa, as I squirm on the ground, my shoulders churning into the carpet.

'Oh no!'

His cigarette is clamped between his in-rolled lips: he gathers my ankles in one big hand, then he turns to leave the cigarette in the ashtray.

'Oh the mouse,' he says. 'Oh the mouse,' and his fingers dance and scrabble across the soft underside of my foot.

Being dead was like being tickled, except that when you flew out of your body you never came back.

WHEN I WAS TWELVE or so, I used to practise astral flying – it must have been a fashion then. I lay on my back in bed, and when I was fully heavy, too heavy to move, I got up, in my mind, and left the house. I went down the stairs and out the front door. I walked or I drifted along the street. If I wanted to, I flew. And I imagined, or I saw, every single detail of the passing world; every fact about the hall or the stairs and the street beyond. The next day I would go out to look for things I had noticed, for the first time, the night before. And I found them, too. Or I thought I had.

The pubs have shut: there are shouts in the distance and the screams of girls. I lean my forehead against the cold glass, as the traffic lights change and change again. It is time for bed. But I don't want to go to bed. I want to keep them company another little while: my father and mother, dispersed as they are along the sweet, bright arc of the dead.

PAPER ROSES

A COUPLE OF MONTHS AGO, I saw Conor on Grafton Street. He was pushing a buggy, which gave me pause, but then I recognised his sister beside him, home from Bondi. He did not seem surprised to see me. He looked up and nodded, as though we had arranged to meet.

His lips were chapped, I noticed. The light was too strong on his face – the way the sun sets straight down Grafton Street – and when we circled around, the better to see each other, I was bizarrely worried that my skin had aged.

'All right. You?'

'Yeah.'

His sister was watching us, with a look so tragic I felt like asking her did the budgie die.

'Oh my goodness!' I said, instead, and I bent down to look under the hood of the buggy. There was her baby, a little shock of humanity, looking me bang in the eye.

'Gorgeous!' I said, and asked how long she was staying, and what the news from Sydney was while Conor seemed more and more tired, just standing there.

After I walked on I got the blip of a text in my pocket.

'Are we married?'

I kept going. I put one foot in front of the other. A second text arrived.

'Need to talk about stuff.' I glanced around then but Conor was thumbs deep in his mobile. Fatter too, in the harsh light. Or, not so much fat as more solid. He glanced up, and I had, as I turned away, an impression of his weight along the length of me, top to toe.

'I'M JUST SAYING,' says Fiachra. 'He's small, good-looking, witty.'

'So?'

'He's your type.'

'I don't have a type.'

'I'm just saying.'

So all right, they are both on the smallish side. They are both good company; both hard to know well. But underneath the charm Conor is an absent-minded sort. And Seán? When the party stops, when the door closes, when the guests go home . . .

They are completely different people. People love Conor, but they do not love Seán. They are attracted to Seán, which is not the same thing. Because Seán has a permanent joke in his eye, and it is usually you – the joke I mean – he is such a tease. And he likes to boast a little. And he likes to do you down.

My grey-haired boy.

He always compliments the thing you don't expect. It is never the thing you made an effort with: the dress, or the jewellery, or the hair. He compliments the thing that is wrong, so it gets more wrong all night.

'What do you think?'

Coming down the stairs, ready to go out: there is something about my expectant look that annoys him.

'I like the lipstick.'

These days, it is always my mouth. I should not have told him about my father in the hospice. I know that now. I tell him less and less.

My poor, raggedy mouth.

Seán Peter Vallely, born 1957, educated to be obnoxious by the Holy Ghost Fathers, reared to be obnoxious by his mother, Margot Vallely, who loved him very much, of course, but was so disappointed he did not grow up tall.

You could be worn out by it, that's all. By this man's inability to lose.

I am only thirty-four. That is what I caught myself thinking. There is still time. There is something the fat on his chest does – I mean, he has very little fat on his chest, and anyway I do not care – but there is something this layer does, the effort it makes, that is dispiriting. And I do not mind until his eyes check me over, like the mirror does not see him.

Then, as though he knows what I am thinking, he says, 'Look at you. You should be out there. You should be.'

'What?'

'I don't know.'

Neither of us can say the word 'baby'.

'I don't want to be out there,' I say. Thinking, *He will use this as an excuse to get rid of me.*

And, *This is one of his tactics too.*

I came in late, one Saturday, after ending up in Reynards talking shite with Fiachra until three in the morning, just like the old days. I stumbled about the bedroom, and there was, I admit, a bit of cavorting as I discarded my clothes, then I jumped into bed and snuggled up.

Seán, who had been asleep, was having none of it. Recollection is dim, but, between one grope and the next, I must have conked out. Only to wake maybe two hours later in such a state of fright, I suspect he shoved me in my sleep. He was lying in the darkness with his eyes open, as he had clearly been doing for some time. He said something – something horrible, I can't remember what it was – and we were in the middle of breaking up; shouting, grabbing dressing gowns, slamming doors. It went from Fiachra to everything, with nothing in-between.

You always.

You never.

The thing about you is.

It was, in a spooky way, just like being married. Though there were, crucially, differences of style. Conor used to take the moral high ground, for example, and Seán doesn't bother – the air up there doesn't suit him, he says. No, Seán doesn't get aggrieved, he gets mean and he gets cold, so I always end up weeping in a different room, or trying to placate him. Sitting in the silence. Lifting my hand to touch him. Putting the work in. I coax him back to me.

Then he gets aggrieved.

Anyway.

Making up is always sweet.

And though I miss the future I might have had, and each and all of Conor Sheils' fat babies, I do not think that we are selfish to want to keep the thing unbroken and beautiful; to hold on to the knowledge that comes when we look into each other's eyes.

I just don't know how to explain it.

I thought it would be a different life, but sometimes it is like the same life in a dream: a different man coming in the door, a different man hanging his coat on the hook. He comes home late, he goes out to the gym, he gets stuck on the internet: we don't spend our evenings in restaurants, or dine by candlelight anymore, we don't even eat together, most of the time. I don't know what I expected. That receipts would not have to be filed, or there would be no such thing as bad kitchen cabinets, or that Seán would switch on a little sidelamp instead of flicking the main switch when he enters a room. Seán exists. He arrives, he leaves. He forgets to ring me when he is delayed, and so the dinner is mistimed: the Butler's Pantry lamb with puy lentils that I heat up in the microwave. He reads the newspaper – quite a lot, actually – and there is nothing so wrong with any of this, but sometimes the intractability of him, perhaps of all men, drives me up the wall.

It's like they don't know you exist unless you are standing there in front of them. I think about Seán all the time when he is gone, about who he is, and where he is, and how I can make things right for him. I hold him in my care. All the time.

And then he walks in the door.

SEÁN IN MY SISTER'S GARDEN in Enniskerry, with his back to me and his face to the view, and the rowan tree at his side has a skipping rope tangled in its branches that are still just twigs.

The day has been warm and I have had a lot of Chardonnay. I am recently back from Australia. I am in love and I am working really hard at the whole Enniskerry thing with the neighbours and the kids. So the man who is standing at the bottom of the garden is just a little rip in the fabric of my life. I can stitch it all up again, if he does not turn around.

Seán stands at the window in his pyjamas, with the frost flowering across the window. Or he stands at the window in the summer light and his naked back is a puzzle of muscle and bone – he still looks like a young man, from behind – and I want to whisper, *Turn around.*

Or, *Don't turn around.*

The weeks I spent waiting for his call, the months I spent waiting for him to leave Aileen. The loneliness of it was, in its own way, fantastic. I lived with it, and danced with it. I brought it to a kind of perfection the Christmas before last, just a few months before he went clear.

The house in Terenure had been on the market four months already, and a flood of people had been through the place, opening cupboards, pulling up the corners of carpets, sniffing the air. My living room, the sofa where I sat, my mother's bed, were all – they still are – on the internet for anyone to click on and dismiss: the stairs we slid down on our bellies, the dark bedroom over the garage, the stain around the light switch. I found a discussion board online where they were laughing at the price – but other than that, it was hard to know what people thought. A single bidder who might have been an investor made a lot of fuss but didn't come through. A married couple with kids offered low, and then faded. And so it was Christmas. My father was not there to ruin the day. My mother was not there to make it all better. My sister was not speaking to me. My lover was in the cold bosom of his family, wearing a paper hat.

I thought about him all day: his daughter sitting at his feet, writing her first ever email, *Hello Daddy!* His wife in the kitchen, her hair drooping in the steam from the brussels sprouts. His wretched mother looking about her with a glittering eye.

I had a pathetic little tree in the corner of the living room, a plastic thing you plug in, with light running to the tips of its fibre-optic needles. I made myself a sandwich for lunch and drank a cup of tea. I thought about leaving the house but I just couldn't. There was traffic on the road outside, but they were all travelling to each other: even the taxi men had their wives beside them and their children in the back seat.

There were times, in the last years of my mother's life, when she could not walk out the front door, and on that day, moving from room to room, I think I understood why. Inside was unbearable, and outside beyond my imagining.

I finally drove into town around two o'clock; where I abandoned the car on a set of double yellow lines. In the windows of the Shelbourne, you could see the respectable flotsam tucking into their hotel turkey, or lifting their heads to look out on deserted streets. I walked past the locked gates of Stephen's Green, down the empty maw of Grafton Street, the mannequins in the shop windows frozen as if to say: this is it! this is the day! I thought, if I fell down in the road, there would be no one to find me until morning. By the wall of Trinity, I passed a tall couple who looked like tourists. They turned their faces as I walked by, chiming, *Happy Christmas*, *Happy Christmas*, and I felt it keenly; the pure shame of it. I did not exist. I would end up breaking windows, just to show that I was real. I would shout his name: my lover who could not risk – he could not risk it! – a text or a call.

I didn't break any windows, of course. I made my way back to the car and drove home. When I checked my phone, I found a message from Fiona. It read, 'Happy Christmas, xxxxxx yr sis' and it made me cry.

In fact something did come through from Seán about seven o'clock. It said, 'Check the shed' where I found a bunch of roses and a slender half-bottle of Canadian ice-wine. And despite the fact that I do not really drink anymore, I ended up drinking the lot of it, following the last sweet drops with a skull-splitting dose of whiskey. None of it was right – the perfect drink does exist, but it is never, somehow, the one you have in your hand. I worked on, nonetheless, until I was steady and empty and clean. The next day I was worried I had made a noise sitting there; some keening, lowing, honk of pain, but I am pretty sure I kept silent, and that when the day was over, the season slaughtered, I managed, with some dignity, to rise and turn and walk upstairs to bed.

I woke up late on Stephen's Day with the headache I so

richly deserved and, after a breakfast of tea and Christmas pudding, I got in the car and crawled out to Fiona's house in Enniskerry. I wept a bit as I drove, and put on the windscreen wipers by accident. I did not call beforehand. I did not know what to say.

It was three o'clock when I arrived and darkness was already in the air. I parked for a moment and saw no sign of life, but my nephew Jack was in the front room and he opened the door before I had the chance to knock. He stared me up and down, wondering how to respond to the amazing fact that I was real. Then he decided on indifference.

'Hi,' he said.

'Hi Jack.' He hung on to the side of the door, staring at me through the gap.

'Where's your Mum?'

'She's upstairs having a cuddle.'

'Right.'

There seemed very little I could say to this, but he had already turned and run back into the front room. The door was still open, so I pushed through into the hall and closed it quietly behind me.

'And where's your sister?' I said, carefully.

'Out.'

'And what are you doing?'

'I'm writing a book,' he said.

He was on his knees in the living room. I thought he might tell me more about it, but he just flopped back down on to the floor and pulled the pages of his copy book into the crook of his arm. He stuck his tongue out of the corner of his mouth and wrote: bum in the air, cheek on the page, eyes inches away from the pen's moving tip.

I sat and watched him for what seemed like a long time. The house was entirely silent. I was about to ask him more questions, when I heard someone come downstairs and go into the back of the house. It was Fiona, I saw her through the connecting doors. She was wearing her dressing gown and she looked, I thought, distinctly rested, you might almost say 'refreshed'. She put the kettle on, then saw me and took fright.

'How long have you been here?'

'I just arrived,' I said.

'Jack, you should always tell me if there's someone at the door. Always, all right?'

'Don't worry,' I said trying to protect him from her.

'Do you hear me, Jack?'

'All right.'

She looked at me and gave a crooked smile.

'You want some tea?'

'WE NEED TO TALK about the house,' I said later when the relief hit.

'Yeah. The house,' she said, and waved a depressed hand in the air. And to be fair to Fiona, she has never been greedy in that way.

'Did I tell you, we sold the place in Brittas?'

'No.'

'Well we did. I'm telling you, nothing is shifting over a million. Nothing. Shay says.'

'Really?' I said.

'Nothing being built. Not one brick, he says, on another brick, this year. Not one.'

'Well it was too mad,' I said. 'Wasn't it?'

'You think?'

And we listen to it for a moment; the rumour of money withering out of the walls and floors and out of the granite kitchen countertops, turning them back to bricks and rubble and stone.

Shay came downstairs, freshly showered and full of himself, in his polo shirt and jeans.

'Gina!' he said, like we were old golfing buddies too long away from the tees. Then he left, at speed, in order to pick up Megan. Fiona started putting a salad together on the kitchen island and I said it was over between myself and Seán. Just in case she wanted to know. Just in case she was interested.

'Finished,' I said. I did not want to see him again. He could go back to his wife.

'What do you mean "go back"?' said Fiona. 'He never left.'

'Whatever.'

'I don't think he even told her, you know?'

'No?'

So I really did mean it, when I said I did not want to see him again – not ever. Seán was three hundred yards down the road, playing the family man, my sister was in her kitchen, playing the perfect wife and I was the perfect fool. There would be penalties, I knew that. Because I really felt, just then, that I had lost the game.

'I don't know what you saw in him,' said Fiona.

'Little fucker,' I said.

'It's just something he does, you know. You're not supposed to take it seriously.'

'Well I did.'

'He sat there,' she said, and she was angry now – whether she was angry with me, or on my behalf, it was hard to tell.

'He sat there,' pointing at a leather tub chair. 'And he told me how lonely he was. No. He told me how lonely his wife was. How worried he was about his wife.'

'When was that?' I said.

Fiona looked at the sheet of glass between the kitchen and the garden, where her reflection was emerging from the dusk. She checked her face, its degree of sadness, and the state of her hair.

'Little fucker,' she said. 'I was fond of him.'

And she leaned over the black granite of her kitchen island, making claws of her upturned hands, the way Seán does, when he is in persuasive mode.

But you know, everyone makes a pass at Fiona, it is the burden she carries through life. Even the postman fancies my sister, she is a martyr to it, she can't even open her own front door.

'When was that?' I said again.

'Oh I don't know,' she said.

And then I remembered something else about my sister. It's not that everyone fancies her, that is not her problem. Her problem is the way they love her. Men. They don't want to shag her so much as pine for her. That is the thing that makes her sad.

'Years ago,' she said. 'I was about two minutes' pregnant

with Jack. I remember, I was really stupid with it. I couldn't figure out what he was saying to me.'

'What did he say?'

'Oh I don't know.' She moves to the double-door fridge that seems to occupy half her kitchen wall. 'What do they ever say?'

She opens it and the plastic seal gives way with a slight sucking sound. She says, 'Gina. You know there's no work for Shay. You know he hasn't worked since October last.'

III

KNOCKING ON HEAVEN'S DOOR

WHEN EVIE WAS FOUR YEARS OLD, she fell off the swing and Aileen slapped the au pair, and Seán, when he arrived home, put his little finger into his daughter's mouth to find where she had bitten the inside of her cheek. He checked her pupils.

'Look at me, Evie. Now look up at the light.'

'I lost my shoe,' she said.

So he went out into the dusk and found the little glittering ballet flat beside the swing. The back of it was smeared with clay, and there was a little divot of turf still attached to the heel.

THERE WAS A TIME, after Fiona's ruthless little anecdote in her kitchen, that I questioned everything that had happened between myself and Seán, down to our choice of bed. I had missed key details, I thought: I had misread the signs. If love is a story we tell ourselves then I had the story wrong. Or maybe passion is just, and always, a wrong-headed thing.

Now, I feel if I can figure out what happened to Evie, I can tell the story properly. If I can think about it and understand it, then I will be able to understand Seán, and ease his pain.

THE EVENING SHE FELL off the swing, they sat with the drained and smiling child in the GP's waiting room, and she turned to her father and said, 'Did I die?'

'Don't be silly,' he said. 'Look at you, you're all alive!'

The doctor, who had a marked English accent, introduced himself as 'Malachy O'Boyle' – a name so makey-uppey and Irish that, Aileen said later, 'it was definitely fake'. He sat Evie up on his examining couch and laid her down. He felt the back of her head, checked her pupils and all her signs, while listening to, and ignoring, Aileen's clear and agitated description of events that afternoon.

'Did she have a temperature?'

'No.'

'Are you sure?' At which Aileen fell silent, because of course, she had not been there.

'So Evie,' he said – now he had dealt with her mother. 'Tell me what happened.'

'I fell off the swing,' she said.

'Anything else?'

'Nope.'

'Good girl,' he said. 'Did anything happen before you fell? What were you looking at?'

She gave him a keen and suspicious glance and said, 'The clouds.'

'Were they nice clouds?'

Evie did not answer. But she did not take her eyes off him,

either then or subsequently, and when, at the end of the consultation, he offered her a lollipop she said, 'No thank you,' which, from her, was a very great insult indeed.

Malachy O'Boyle sat back in his swivel chair and, in his easy, adenoidal way, told them Evie had bumped her head, and that she would be fine. It was also possible, he thought, that she had suffered an event, a convulsion or seizure, what people used to call a fit. He was by no means sure of this, and even if she had, most children who do never have a second one. But just so they were aware of it. Just so they could keep an eye.

They left his room and they paid the receptionist fifty-five euros. Then they went out to the car. Aileen said, 'We are going to casualty.' She was white and trembling in the passenger seat beside him. Seán said, 'It's Friday evening.'

But they went to casualty, and they sat in casualty for four-and-a-half hours, in order to be seen by a tired girl in a white coat who repeated pretty much what the fake-Irish GP had said. The girl, who looked about sixteen, resisted all talk of seizures and MRI scans, allowed that she could keep Evie in for observation but it would have to be on a trolley. And so they sat, or paced, or stood beside the trolley where Evie slept the delicious, heartbreaking sleep of a child, while, all around them, Friday-night Dublin wept, bled and cursed (and that was just the porters, as Aileen tartly said). They had one plastic chair between them. From time to time, Seán bent over the end of his daughter's mattress, and set his head on his folded arms, where he lurched asleep for thirty seconds at a time.

They stayed, itching with tiredness, until, at ten o'clock in the morning, a more important-looking doctor swept past, checked the metal clipboard, pulled Evie's eyelids open, one at a time, and with a breezy bit of banter, gave them all permission to go home. They had no idea who he was – as Aileen pointed out later, he might have been a cleaner in drag – but they were, by this stage, pliable, grateful, almost animal. All their normal human competency was gone. The rules had changed.

Aileen swung, in the next while, from efficiency to uselessness. She bullied or she froze; there was nothing in-between. She became convinced, after many late nights on various websites, that there was something seriously wrong. Evie had been crying out in her sleep for months – perhaps a year – before she fell off the swing, and sometimes they found her confused and on her bedroom floor. Aileen dragged the child around three different GPs ('The medical equivalent of a stage mother,' as Seán described her), until she got a referral for a paediatric neurologist with a two-month waiting list, and that night she got, for the first time since he had known her, rat-arsed on champagne.

Meanwhile, the au pair did not so much leave as flounce out, and although they needed another, and urgently, Aileen stalled at the idea of ringing the agency again. She took half days off work, and sometimes made Seán take the other half, she rang neighbours and got babysitters in. The childcare, which had been until then a smooth enough affair – at least as far as he was concerned – became insoluble. It was as though she did not want it to work, he realised, one day when the handover went astray, and she ended up screaming down the phone at him: *You said two o'clock but you meant three o'clock. How many lies is that? How many lies are there, in a whole fucking hour?*

The guilt and the worry had overwhelmed her, she said later. She just wanted to stay with Evie, all the time.

And Seán said, 'She's fine.'

IT HAPPENED AT BREAKFAST TIME. Evie was always a joy in the morning – 'You put them to bed screaming,' Seán said, 'and they wake up all new.' Evie sat up in bed at first light and read a book – or just talked to the pictures – then got up at the sound of the alarm clock to slip between her waking parents. She talked non-stop, she wandered and chatted and got distracted. Her mornings were spent in a state of loveliness and forgetting: looking in her wardrobe and not remembering to dress, helping to make the porridge then letting it go cold, trying to walk out the door before she had located her shoes.

On this morning, she was neglecting her porridge for a black-and-white stuffed hen, which she danced across the table with squawks and cluckings, in the middle of which she rolled her eyes back and slid on to the floor. Seán watched her for many seconds before he even tried to make sense of what was happening. Under the table, Evie shook and rattled. Her eyes were open and fixed. She didn't look at him, but at the wall behind her head, and what disturbed Seán, in retrospect, was the gentle, thoughtful look he saw in her eyes, like someone examining the idea of pain. Her hands were clenched, her right foot throbbed or kicked, and it seemed to him that her body was outraged by her brain's betrayal, and was fighting to regain control. This was an illusion, he knew, but nothing could quite convince Seán that Evie was not suffering. She made small mewling sounds, as tiny and uncomprehending as when she was newborn, and her mouth drooled and snapped.

Aileen had pulled the chair back, to give her space. She stood over her daughter. Then she ducked down quickly to cushion her head from the hard tiles.

'Don't,' said Seán, who had some idea that Evie should not be touched, at all.

'Don't what?'

Aileen's calm was almost unnatural. She held her daughter by the shoulders, then slipped easily on to the floor and set Evie's head on her lap, reaching up to hold on to the tabletop with her free hand.

Seán remembered this image with great clarity: the unflattering fold of fat between her knee and thigh, and Aileen, usually so fastidious, with drool smearing her skirt. Meanwhile, Evie's clenched hands pumped more slowly, and her lips seemed almost blue.

She was not breathing, he thought.

Evie bucked and bucked and then stopped. She looked as though she had forgotten something. Then, after a moment of great emptiness, her body pulled in a rasping breath. After this came another breath. Aileen rubbed and patted her, making soothing, whimpering sounds and it took a long time to bring the child back to herself – or perhaps none of it took a long time, perhaps the whole thing happened in a very short time; it just felt endless and messy. Evie was confused, Aileen was confused, calling her name, rubbing her back and arms. And then, something shifted and caught.

Evie sat up. She roared. She struggled out of her mother's restraining arms; outraged, calling the world to account.

HE WAS SO PROUD of her.

There are times when Seán seems to blame me for the failure of his marriage, but he never blames me for what happened to Evie. I coaxed it all out of him on the car journeys we took down to the west; the beautiful small roads along the Shannon beyond Limerick: Pallaskenry, Ballyvogue, Oola, Foynes. We drove with the wide river showing through sun-dappled trees; Seán concentrating on the driving, me safely dressed, neither of us looking at the other, sitting side by side.

Talking about her makes him simple. Seán, a man, as he would himself admit, addicted to winning and to losing – when Evie got ill, all that fell away, and the world opened up to them in a way that amazes him yet.

THE MORNING EVIE HAD THE SEIZURE, Aileen rang the neurologist's office where they had an appointment in a fortnight's time. They were on their way into casualty. Aileen was in the back of the car, holding Evie around her seat belt, and managing the phone. The doctor's secretary said, 'Hang on a minute,' and she put her hand over the mouthpiece. Then she came back on to say, 'Dr Prentice will send down the team.'

'Sorry?'

'When you come to casualty. Dr Prentice will see you after you talk to her team.'

And she did.

It was, for those first few hours, a kind of bliss. A doctor, two doctors, a bed in the day ward. The consultant arrived; a small, profoundly powerful woman, trussed up in a navy crêpe suit. The consultant was kind. She allowed for an MRI scan and an EEG. She used the word 'benign', which made them think about brain tumours. She wrote a prescription. She said a lot of nice and reassuring things, many of which were hard to remember.

They walked the hospital corridors looking for an exit, with Evie still exhausted in her father's arms, and they felt – at least Seán felt – the heaviness and beauty of her head, as it rolled on his shoulder, the mystery of bringing her into the world, and the way she escaped the mystery by being so absolutely and pragmatically herself. They looked around them, memorising their future in this place: the signed football jerseys in their frames, the wire games on wooden tables, and yellowing murals of cartoon characters long gone out of fashion. A cleaner asked were they lost, which they were. A passing nurse said, 'Do you know your way out?' There were only two kinds of people in this place – people who were nice, and people who were lost. They held hands. They had never been closer; heading for the swing doors of the children's hospital and the daylight beyond.

For the next several months they bought and wrangled their way up the waiting lists and the house was run according to Evie's medical schedule. They rose in darkness, wrapped her in a blanket and carried her to the car. Seán drove as the dawn slipped down the hillsides, filling the bowl of Dublin Bay with a pale mist, and the sun rose out of the sea in front of them, washed and white. In the hospital, Evie was hot and damp and delicious to the touch, as they carried her down one corridor or another to the right waiting room, or the wrong one, where nice people (they were all nice, all of them) took their paper-work or redirected them, and they walked on, looking through the glass panel on each door in case they should stumble into a ward where the bald children were, or the children with scars too big for their small bodies: all the hopeful little freaks. Very quickly, they stopped seeing the children's diseases and saw them as real children, and this frightened them too: the idea that this reversal of nature could be an ordinary thing. They did not look at their own reflections. Not ever. Each sick, or even dying, child – beautiful as a flower – seemed to be attached to some unwashed parent, who slept on the floor, and forgot to get her roots done, and looked like a refugee.

After the first few appointments, Aileen said there was no point in the pair of them spending their lives down there, she could manage on her own. Then, when the tests were clear, she threw it back at him, saying, 'You couldn't even come to the hospital, you weren't even there.'

It was the relief that made her shout. The diagnosis, when it came, was very terrible, or very hopeful – it was hard to say which. Dr Prentice said that Evie would, in all probability, grow out of the seizures. She did not have a tumour, she would probably not die – unless in her sleep, suddenly, for no reason at all: unless in the bath, or under a car, or in their living room, if she had a seizure while standing beside the fire. There was nothing wrong with her, she seemed to say, except for this thing that was wrong with her. The medication was presented as a choice: seizures or no seizures, you decide.

'Most people,' said Dr Prentice, in her kind, crisp way, 'opt for the latter.'

The pills made Evie confused – at least Aileen thought so. A contented, almost biddable child, she got frustrated and threw tantrums, even in the morning – when all that lovely forgetting was now turned into something more sinister. Aileen thought she might be having hallucinations.

'You think?' said Seán.

It was hard to tell. The child was four years old: she spent her day in a state of constant imagining. But Aileen said she stopped dead in the street, or startled at nothing. Every so often, she lifted a hand as though brushing cobwebs from in front of her eyes. She said strange things. Aileen did not know if this was some kind of shadow of the seizures that had now stopped, or a side effect of the pills she took to stop them. Seán privately thought it was a symptom of Aileen's anxiety, but they both listened to Evie's prattle with a more attentive ear.

After months of this fretfulness and concern, and many hundreds of hours on the internet, Aileen decided to take Evie off her medication.

'I want my little girl back,' she said.

Aileen's worry had become impossible. She had worried so hard and for so long, it had transcended itself and turned into a rapture of care.

'It's not her anymore,' she said. 'It's not Evie.'

Seán argued that the child was only four: 'She's changing every minute,' he said. 'She's never the same.'

To which Aileen answered, '*How can you not know?*'

So Evie was weaned off her tablets and the seizure, when

it happened, was almost a relief, after so many days of waiting for it to come. Days and weeks of being present and mindful, waiting for the crackle in her brain, fearful of the shadows, as the sun was cut to flitters by the roadside trees. Do you smell something, Evie? Do you see something? What are you thinking, Evie?

It happened in the crèche where Evie now spent her days. The woman in charge didn't seem to bat an eyelid. It was an event. She had managed it.

'I just held her in my arms,' she said. 'Poor little mite.'

Not that they liked her for it.

'What a cow,' said Aileen, because reality had shifted for them, one more time. They were now looking at a world in which an absent, juddering child was a normal thing. Their child. Their beautiful, ever-present Evie.

There is no doubt that Aileen, who was above all things rational, was not behaving rationally when she decided to put an end to this nonsense, once and for all. She put Evie on a diet. It was a medical diet. The hospital they attended did not supervise it, but some hospitals did, she said, though it was usually for children much worse off than Evie. It was a ketogenic regime – like Atkins but weirder and stricter – it seemed to involve endless but very exact amounts of whipped cream. No carbohydrates were allowed. None whatsoever. Not an apple, not the stain of sauce on a baked bean. One crisp and the child would be foaming at the mouth and falling under the nearest bus, no question.

Seán should have argued it out, he said. Or he should have talked to her more – Aileen that is – made her feel less lonely in it. But it was all unstoppably itself, he thought. And there was nothing so terribly wrong with whipped cream. So he just let her at it.

The diet never worked. At least, Evie never stuck to it – Seán suspected, besides, that the crèche woman was feeding her Hula Hoops, out of sympathy. They started fresh every Monday, by Thursday Evie would be discovered with sugar on her breath. Aileen would go into the next room in order to compose herself, then she would come back to discuss things with Evie.

'Remember, Mrs Mooch, how we talked about your brain?'

One evening, after finding a nest of peach stones stuffed down the back of the sofa, Aileen stood and wept. They were turning their daughter into a failure, she said; their fabulous daughter, who was now a constant disappointment to them; also, when it came to food, an accomplished thief and liar. And though Aileen saw all this happening, she did not know how to fix it, and there was nothing Seán could do except stand outside the circle and tell her that everything was going to be all right when it was not all right. It was all impossible. And it was all her fault.

It was during this phase of their lives, the ketogenic phase, that I saw Seán for the first time, standing at the bottom of my sister's garden in Enniskerry. I do not know what he was thinking about. He might have been thinking about Evie, or about work, or about a woman at work. He might have been admiring the view, or wondering how much the houses were worth, between here and the sea. Perhaps he was pining for my sister

Fiona, who is so pretty and sad. Or he might have been thinking about nothing. The way men often claim to do.

'What are you thinking about?'

'I don't know. Nothing much.'

It is fairly clear, however, that he was not thinking about Evie in any practical way, because, when she came up behind him there was a stolen smear of something sticky and very purple on her little face.

He said, 'Oh for God's sake, Evie,' and he sighed. He watched Aileen scrub at the gunk with a paper napkin, then he looked over to me.

Of course, I know Evie's story mostly from Seán's point of view, and I know that Seán does not always tell the truth. Or he does not remember the truth. The way he tells it, he met Fiona's sister (as he used to think of me) for the first time, walking in Knocksink woods, with the kids up to their knees in muck. He has no recollection of me at the party, standing by the fence.

But whatever way he remembers it, there is something in Evie's story that Seán is constantly trying to understand. Something about himself, perhaps.

And then there is Aileen.

Evie marched into Terenure – quite early on – and handed me a battered-looking envelope, then she rolled her eyes, and clumped off to switch on Joan's crap little TV. Inside was an information sheet, headed 'What to Do When Someone has an Epileptic Seizure'. This was clipped to a pathetic note from Aileen – typed, unsigned – that began, 'When Evie was four years old, she was diagnosed as suffering from benign rolandic epilepsy of childhood (BREC). Recently that diagnosis has been under review.' I read it all. I didn't understand a word of it. I said to Seán, 'So what exactly is wrong with her?'

'Actually nothing,' he said. 'She's fine.'

EVIE, STILL OFF THE MEDICATION, went to school the autumn after the party in Enniskerry, and Aileen had a whole new reality check. The very nice and very young teacher listened to her tale and blinked twice. She said, 'Could you run that by me again?' Seán and Aileen then spoke to the headmistress who was completely reassuring. She also reminded them, on their way out the door, that there were twenty-nine other children in Evie's class.

In October, Evie had a seizure in the line before the bell went, and everyone made a great fuss of her. But there was one little girl who was mean and really, as Evie said to her mother, with all the wisdom a five-year-old can muster, 'It's just not me, you know?'

They laughed when she said it, but they were ashamed too. Evie was saying that this might happen inside her, but she was outside it. It was not for her a question of poetry, or personality. It was just a bad thing that happened to her and she wanted it to stop.

They had to admire the person she was, at five years old, and hope she never lost it. Aileen relented. They put her on a different drug which slowly made her fat and, perhaps – again it was hard to tell – a bit incontinent. The seizures stopped. All her loopiness faded away. If anything, she seemed a little dull, though that might have been an illusion of her new girth – and besides, she was growing up. Also out. By the time I saw her in Brittas she was a different person. This time it was Seán who had put the child on a diet – for looking, I suspect, *less than middle class.* He saw it as a simple balance to her medication, but it is possible that Evie irritated him more, the larger she grew. Because the forbidden ice-pop that day in Brittas had a kind of despair built into it – the way they clung together – both of them hanging on to Evie's disappearing childhood, there on Fiona's deck.

That autumn, at Dr Prentice's suggestion, they tapered the dose, and then, finally, gave it up. Nothing happened.

Evie was absolutely herself – body and mind. She was a little private, perhaps; watchful and solitary. There was, when I met her upstairs on New Year's Day, a stilled and expectant look, like a child who has known danger, or one who is slightly deaf. She continued free of seizures: her childhood illness was now finished. In a way, it had never been very terrible. She had suffered, the summer of the whipped cream diet, four or five major seizures. Her last was the one in the yard, the year she started school. She did not have another problem until she was ten years old.

AND THAT, SO FAR as I can tell it, is what happened to Evie. But it is not the whole truth. It is just the truth in a concentrated form.

Because, let's face it – from the day the child was born, Aileen acted as though Evie could die at any moment. What she discovered, when she looked into the baby's muddy blue eyes, was fear in a form she had never known before. And weaning Evie off her medication was easy compared to weaning her off the breast, for example, which was a major production only slightly less fraught than the three-act opera of getting her on the tit in the first instance.

But though you might think Aileen pushed him away, it is also true, if you do the dates (which I have), if you work the connections and listen to the silences, that Seán had knocked out at least one affair before Evie fell off the swing and battered her little heels on the ground. This is the real way it happens, isn't it? I mean in the real world there is no one moment when a relationship changes, no clear cause and effect.

Or the effect might be clear, the cause is harder to trace.

The effect walks up, many years later, when you are out to dinner with your new partner and she says, 'My goodness. Would you look who it is.'

I think his first affair was with the Global Tax woman, the one on the conference in Switzerland. Going by the dates, she was, at a guess, a series of horrible, hot little encounters when Evie was in nappies. The little window in his heart, that opened in Fiona's kitchen, when she was just pregnant with Jack – that was when Evie was three. So if he talked to Fiona about the sadness of his wife, that day, then maybe his wife had good reason to be sad. Unless she wasn't sad, of course, and he was just looking for something to say.

Bubblegum girl, as I like to think of her, the one with the nail varnish and the B in Honours Maths, was drinking like a twenty-two-year-old and hanging out of railings around the time I met him in Brittas Bay. I think about his body on the beach, and it seems different to me now. His strong legs and neat back standing at the edge of the sea, while his wife disentangled herself from Evie on the strand: the tufty nipples he covered up with a black T-shirt, while we sat and talked, it all seems, now, differently naked; shadowed by another girl's touch, wrapped in her secret arms. Cocky little bastard. No wonder he leaned back on his elbows like that and lifted his face to the sky.

I don't know why I should worry about his infidelities to Aileen especially considering that I was one of them. I should take it as proof that he never loved her, though I think he really did love her once. Did he love my sister that day in Brittas? Or all of these women, all of the time? I don't care.

He loves me now. Or he loves me too.

Or.

I love him. And that is as much as any of us can know.

THE THINGS WE DO FOR LOVE

THE FIRST THING I HEAR in the morning is the phone.

'Are you going into work?' It is Seán.

'I think so.'

'Right,' he says. 'Thanks.'

'Where are you?' I say, but he is gone.

Neither is he, as I discover when I let the phone fall back on the duvet, in the bed beside me. It is half past eight. There is something too blank about the light outside. I get up into the murk of the room, and pull the curtains of grey linen, and find the world flattened by monochrome.

I do the winter sprint around the freezing room, shower and dress, pick the phone up to find a text:

'Can you pick Ev up from Foxrock?'

To which I reply, 'Hve meeting. Walking into town.'

I can't imagine how Evie is supposed to get out of Enniskerry, which must be snowed in. The schools are closed. I don't see any cars on the road, and the television, when I turn it on, has pictures of frozen confusion, quiet chaos. Nothing is moving, except makeshift toboggans and snowballs.

You would think that on this day of all days, she would just stay at home. But I know nothing about these things – the reason Evie stays, or the reasons she goes – there are deep forces at work, great imperatives. We must inch forward massively, like rock along a fault line, for fear of the quake.

At ten thirty, another, somewhat redundant, text from Seán, 'Hang on . . .'

'Bated breath,' I write – and then delete.

Since his daughter came into my house, life is one long wrangle about arrangements: times, places, pick-ups, drop-offs, handovers. And everything has to be done in person. For some reason, you can't just ask someone – friend's mother, drama teacher or whoever – to put the child in a taxi. I mean, how much is my time worth? How much is Seán's time worth? Surely more than the tenner for the fare. But you can't put daughters in taxis. Putting a daughter in a taxi is like asking a foreigner to molest her, *on the meter*.

'Meet Ev 3.30ish Dawson St??'

'ok. When home?'

'145 bus stop.'

'whn home?'

'trying!!!!'

'How Buda?'

He does not reply.

I have saved this man's life, but there are things I am not allowed to – that I do not need to – know. The money thing, for example. I don't know whether he can break even in Budapest, or what is happening to his house by the beach, which is now up for sale too. I think, to be fair, he doesn't know either. I mean, it's fine. Everything is fine, just so long as no one blinks, no one moves. Meanwhile, it is there on the web for everyone to click over and ignore – the shells on the windowsills in Ballymoney, and whether Clonskeagh has gone Sale Agreed. Myself and Seán have loved a whole litter of For Sale signs into being. And no one is about to buy anything. Not in this snow.

At eleven my meeting calls to cancel, as I knew she would. I hold my phone and look at it, wondering who to text about what. Then I just put it away.

The craziest thing, I think, is the way I can't speak to them in person, to Aileen or to Evie. I am a grown woman with a job and a salary, and I am not allowed talk to the people who, at a whim, make or ruin my Saturdays. I can not even lift the phone.

As I say to Fiachra, it's like I get all the stupid stuff and none of the cuddles. Not that I want the cuddles: Evie (am I the only one who notices this?) is no longer a child.

She is nearly twelve. Evie had a growth spurt last autumn and, though she measured herself against her father – chin! earlobe! forehead! – to her preening delight and his seeming pride, it has not yet translated into actual cubic centimetres: this of girl and this of air. She has not yet learned the extent of herself.

So she sits on her father's knee, or rather plonks herself on to his lap, just as she always used to, 'Oh God. Evie,' while he pulls back to guard the family jewels and ducks to the side to keep her skull from breaking his nose. You can't actually see him behind her large and white and radiant flesh. She is dressed like a girl you see throwing up into a litter bin on a Saturday night, in black ripped tights under denim shorts (Aileen looks in the cheap shops to see what she will wear and tries to match it in something a little more expensive), and she really is sitting *on* him as opposed to perching on his knee, and the two of them are entirely happy and natural with this, until they aren't.

'Off now, Evie.'

'Aw-ww.'

'Off!'

Sometimes he succeeds, and sometimes, he lets her stay. Her face in front of his is rounder, the lips softer, and her eyes, though the same shape and colour, are spookily not the same: there is an entirely different human being in there. She swings a leg and looks airily about, claiming her father against all comers, while I sit and smile.

The first time she stayed over I kept away, walking the streets of Galway in the rain, only driving home when I was sure she would be gone. It was September. The house had been on the market exactly a year. If you listened to the car radio, all the money in the country had just evaporated, you could almost see it, rising off the rooftops like steam. And there she was, this cuckoo, sitting in my kitchen; the price I had to pay for love.

The absurdity of it was lost on Seán, who was – who continues to be – completely helpless when it comes to Evie. He can see nothing but her.

So I did not ask his permission the next weekend, but walked in at two o'clock to find the two of them sitting down to lunch.

'Hi!' I said, brightly.

Evie ignored me, but it is possible she ignores everyone for the first while.

Her father said, 'Evie,' and she looked up with hurt eyes. 'You remember Gina.'

'Hm,' she said.

And I moved quietly about as she picked through the home-made burger; removing lettuce and cucumber, complaining there was no ketchup, piling on the mayonnaise.

Since then, she comes quite often. We meet in passing. I dodge her rage. I am always brief. I am always nice. I sleep with her father, while she sleeps across the landing. All the doors are open in case she dies in her sleep, even though she is not going to die in her sleep. But I do not think we would make love if they were closed, not even silently.

I come out in the morning, to find her already occupying the bathroom, or she barges past, in some tatty flannelette of infant pink. Every time I see her, she has grown – but massively. It is like a different stranger to bump into every week.

At night, I hear them moving about the spare room, the curtains pulled, the quiet chat as she arranges fluffy toys and night lights and who knows what, until her father – Evie is nearly twelve, remember – lies down beside her and murmurs her to sleep. As often as not he falls asleep too, and I can not tap on the door, or put my head round it to rouse him: I can not risk it. So they lie, cocooned and hopeless and completely contented, while I sit and watch crap TV.

She started coming in September and they ran out of trips and excursions by the middle of October, so they linger in the house and fail to make decisions; Evie whining, *I just want to hang out with my frie-ends.*

For a man who is crazy about his daughter, Seán spends a lot of time telling her to go away. Maybe all parents do this.

'Go and do something,' he says, as she peers over his shoulder at his laptop screen, eating an apple beside his ear. 'What are you standing there for?' He sends her down to the shops for sweets, and then tells her she can't have sweets. He sends her down to the shops for a smoothie, instead. He says, 'Go and play,' when there is no one for her to play with. He tells her to go and read a book, though he never reads books, himself; I have never seen him with a book in his hand. So she plays Nintendo, and then he tells her not to play so much Nintendo.

'Stop touching things, Evie.'

There is no stilling her hands, always on the mooch.

I noticed this the first time we went outside the house together, and walked down to Bushy Park with Evie's new dog (the dog is another story: let me not begin to discuss the dog). She followed each wall with the tips of her fingers, smooth or rough; let them drift through hedges and drag the leaves off bushes.

It was as though she was testing the edges of her world; finding the point where objects began and space stopped.

'There is no need to touch the wall, Evie.'

Seán seemed worried she would shred the pads on her fingers – and there was something else there too, some idea of contamination; whether she would dirty things or be made dirty by them – Seán is, as we know, a clean sort and Evie plays with his disgust in the smallest ways. She doesn't do anything truly taboo, she wouldn't get away with it; she is, besides, at a modest age. Delicate to a fault about her galloping physicality, she never discusses sex and thinks adults are completely gross when they try.

'Oh pull-ease.'

But she scratches her scalp into the fold of a book. She leaves sticky smears on the keyboards and remotes and phones. She twirls her hair, or sucks her hair, she is hugely uncomfortable in her bra – for which she has my sympathy, it's a life sentence – and her underwear is constantly prised out and readjusted. She also – and this gets to me too – hoiks the phlegm up her nose instead of using a hanky.

It is all, in its way, fantastic for being so effective. Although she seems to be helpless to it, and maybe she is, it is also the best and quickest way to drive her father around the bend.

'Evie, please!'

'What?'

She also knows, as though by the fruit of long contemplation, the exact and simplest way to his heart. Not just by looking at him with her grey eyes, which should be enough for anyone, which is almost enough for me. Not just by doing well in school and being ostentatiously averse to boys. No, Evie has made friends with the richest girl in the class. Which in Evie's class, out in County Wicklow, is pretty damn rich. In fact, the father of Evie's best friend (blonde, like her mother, with beautiful slim knees) owns houses and hotels, owns whole apartment blocks, from Tralee to Riga.

Her name – and you have to admire her parents for this – is Paddy.

They are doing a project together on lice in horses. Paddy is supplying the horses. I did not ask if Evie was supplying the lice.

AND SOMETIMES, TOO, they are perfect: sitting on the sofa watching 'Father Ted', or out in the open air, or the way they talk in the car, because talking is what Seán is good at, and with his daughter there is no charm and no blame, there is just Seán. I listen to the ease of his tone with her and I think, *He does not speak that way to me.*

He does not hold me by the hand. He does not tickle me, quickly, to get me out of his way. He does not tango me down the hall, and arch me over, backwards. He does not wake in the night, thinking of me.

I have saved his life.

From what?

'You have saved my life,' he said.

But if you ask me, it's not one woman or another that is the saving of Seán. It is the woman he loves but can never desire. It is Evie.

'Take those earphones off, Evie.'

Evie absent or dreaming in front of a screen or a book. Evie failing to focus up, to move along, to snap to.

Evie stalled in front of the mirror for hours at a time, sprouting hair and neuroses, moody as all get out. And it seems so unfair, to be jumping with hormones when you're still in Hello Kitty pyjamas; it is like no one is telling the truth, or no one knows what truth to tell.

I walked in on her one evening. Evie always leaves the

door open when she is in the bath – *You still alive in there, Evie: you haven't gone down the plughole?* Usually, she chats away – just the feel of the warm water seems to set her rattling on – and her father leaves her to it; listening, or pretending to listen, stretched out on our bed across the landing.

But this one evening, she had fallen silent and, between one sentence and the next, I walked in the door.

Evie pulled the sponge up to cover her little budding chest and looked at me with huge grey eyes.

'Don't mind me!' I said, as I dodged across the room to get the thing I needed, whatever it was, from out of the bathroom cabinet.

In the autumn, Evie seemed to get rounder and rounder, fatter and fatter, after which came the amazing stretch and boi-oi-oinngg of this extra flesh into a waist and hips and breasts – though, as I recall, breasts don't feel like fat, at that age, they feel like tenderised gristle. But they look, from what I saw in the bath, heartbreaking and simple.

There is nothing worse than being nearly twelve.

Evie is at that moment. Her body is at that moment when it is wrong to look at her, wrong to think about her nakedness, when it would be criminal to take a photograph. Her body is becoming her own. Her body is becoming lonely. Her father, who used to bathe and dry her, now stretched out staring at the ceiling, across the hall.

'Have you rinsed, Evie? Rinse till you hear it squeak.'

He was off the bed and standing in the doorway when I came out of the bathroom. I lifted my hands in a mock shrug – because all this was normal too – and he nodded and turned away.

And I am suddenly passionate about Evie. I want to take him by the shoulders and explain that my jealousy is a kind of loving, too. Because, when I was her age, my father was sitting up in his hospice bed enjoying the fact that all women were equally nameless to him now.

'Hello my darlings, to what do I owe the pleasure?'

I want to tell him that Evie is lucky to have him, that he, Seán, is where all her luck resides. Because after Miles died nothing went right, unless we made it right; all blessings and bounty, all unexpected joys, came from his love – pathetic as it sometimes was and sometimes huge. After Miles died, everything was hard work – marrying Conor, marrying Shay – and nothing came to either of his daughters gratis and undeserved.

I cried that night. I don't know if Evie heard me; the strange woman weeping beside her father in this strange house. I smothered most of it in the pillow; Seán's hand stroking my back. Me saying, 'I'm sorry, I'll be all right. I'm sorry.'

There she was at breakfast, an overgrown child again; her white arse hanging out of her pink pyjamas. She picked the nuts out of her muesli, and left them on the table in a little heap beside the bowl.

Seán said, 'Eat your breakfast, Evie.'

I said, 'Would you like some eggs?'

And Evie said, 'I hate eggs.'

AND YET, IF IT HAD not been for Evie, we would not be here. That's what I think.

I kissed her father, upstairs in his own house, and Evie

lifted her flapping hands from her sides and she ran over to us saying, 'Happy New Year, Daddy!' and he bent to kiss her too.

As far as Seán was concerned, nothing happened that day. Keep it simple and you will win, or if you don't win – as he liked to say – at least it will be simple. But, sometime after that kiss, between one hotel afternoon and the next hotel afternoon, Evie started to disappear.

How such a constantly tended child could do such a thing, is hard to say. For the first long while, they did not even notice; it crept up on them. Evie was just not where she was supposed to be. She seemed to get lost on her way up the stairs. She didn't show up for meals, only to be found in her bedroom, or the au pair's room, or out in the garden with no coat. One day, around the time my mother died, she failed to arrive back from Megan's house. This was a journey of some three hundred yards down a country road that even Evie was allowed to take by herself.

'When did she leave?' said Aileen to Fiona on the phone: two families streaming out of their separate houses, climbing into four different cars, reversing out of their driveways at a clip. They found her almost immediately. She was standing on the side of the road, as though at an imaginary bus stop, with no sense that her journey had been interrupted, or had taken too long.

'What are you doing Evie?'

'I was just looking.'

It was, up to a point, just the way she was. *Stop dawdling, Evie.* From the time she was three years old, Evie could never get out of a car without pausing endlessly before the jump.

Thresholds made her stall. All journeys were difficult, not for her, but for the people around her, who could never quite figure out just how she managed to slow everything down.

Come along, Evie. So this was nothing more than another failure, on her part, to grow up. Then, one day, she wandered from her mother in the Dundrum Shopping Centre and when Aileen, frantic, found her outside by the fountains, she could not say where she had been.

'I was just,' she said. 'I don't know.'

Seán was in no position to believe that there was a problem. His life with me had taken on some importance, by then; he was a man trying to keep his balance. He was, besides, 'Just not going to do it, this time round.' And though he discussed Evie with me over the phone in those long drifting days after Joan died, he didn't – he just couldn't – listen to Aileen, when the panic machine ground into gear again.

'She's fine,' he said. 'She's just growing. It's fine.'

Then, one Saturday after the summer holidays, Evie did not come out of her drama class. Seán who was doing the pick-up waited, and checked his watch. He went inside where the teacher was packing up and discovered that Evie, though dropped at the door, had not showed up in class that day. They started to ransack the building, the two of them – then Seán decided to try outside. He ran into the street and up the hill, past buildings and doors and girls smoking at the bus stop, into the shopping centre, where he went down the first escalator he came to and stood in the middle of the atrium, and he looked up at a changed world, one full of angles, doors and possibilities that he had never seen before.

He wanted to shout her name and then did not shout. He found a security guard, who muttered into his walkie-talkie, then wrote out a phone number and advised him to ring the local police. Which Seán did, standing on the street, watching buses and cars, and old ladies with stand-up trolleys, going about their usual business. The man who answered asked him to hold the line. Then a woman's voice. I must sound bad, he thought, if they are handing me to a girl.

'Can you describe your daughter?'

Just the word 'daughter', the way she said it, made him feel like a liar. He felt like someone who was about to be found out.

'She has big eyes,' he said.

There was a silence at the other end of the line.

'Take your time, sir. Can you tell me the colour of her eyes?' At which point he did that thing; he turned himself into a person who can describe his daughter in words you might hear on the evening news: age, height, hair colour.

'What was she wearing?'

'I'll have to ring her mother,' he said. And as soon as he cut the connection, Aileen was on the line.

For a few moments, he failed to understand, not just the words she was saying, but her voice itself – she might have been talking Danish – then he somehow figured out that Evie had rung Aileen, or Aileen had rung Evie, and she was in the theatre, where she was supposed to have been all along.

'You spent the class in the toilet?' To which Evie replied, 'No!' And then, 'I must have done.'

There was nothing for it, but to go back to the doctors –

the same round of referrals and endless waiting lists, the same watchfulness and morning anxiety, Aileen on the internet every night, googling 'absences', 'lesions', 'puberty'; inviting it all in.

When they finally found themselves back with Dr Prentice – it was with difficulty, Aileen said, that she did not 'fall on the woman's neck' – Evie had very little to say.

She answered all the questions and gave no clues.

'And what do you think is going on, Evie?' the doctor finally said, to which Evie offered the idea that her brain might be funny.

'In what way funny?'

Evie, who by this time knew more than most children about the human brain, said, 'The two halves – the hemispheres, you know? – it is like they don't join up properly.'

Dr Prentice pursed her mouth and looked into her lap,then she lifted her head and with great clarity and tactfulness, discussed the anomalies of Evie's case, and suggested – strongly suggested – that *alongside* her medical tests and enquiries, they should bring Evie for 'psychiatric assessment'.

This was what was going on, the Christmas I wandered the deserted city streets. They gave her a computer, and told her not to spend so much time on the computer, and they pulled crackers, and hugged her, taking careful turns.

It is my suspicion that, after this, Aileen finally confronted Seán with all the things she had known – but not let herself know – for years. I suspect that she kicked him out. Because she realised the lies they told each other were wrecking Evie's head.

Or perhaps he kicked himself out, for much the same reason.

It is hard to pin down. Seán tells the story differently every time, and he believes it differently each time. But the fact seems to be that, at a time when it seemed most important, for Evie's sake, that they should stay together, it was also vital, for Evie's sake, that they should part.

In the last days of March, they sat in a room full of ghastly china figurines and discussed their daughter with a lemur of a woman – all eyes, and quick little hands – who had been seeing Evie, at great expense, for the previous two months. She looked at them and twitched her head sideways.

'Now. Let's talk about you guys, OK?'

Not OK.

And sometime in the next week, Seán Vallely walked out of his house with nothing, not even a jacket, and he drove, in the middle of the night, to my door.

It was a weeknight: some normal night without him. It might have been two in the morning. I woke to the sound of the bell and the rattle of the letter box. Seán was crouched down, saying my name, trying not to wake the neighbours.

I was not quite awake, myself. I thought someone had died. Then I remembered that Joan was already dead: I had no one left, now, except Fiona. So it was my sister, then – though it seemed so unlikely; Fiona was not, somehow, the dying type. I pulled the door open and he was standing outside in the weather. And the first thing I said was, 'Is she dead?'

'Let me in, will you?'

'Oh, sorry.'

He came inside the door – not very far – he crossed the

threshold and then he leaned back against the wall. Every bit of his face was wet, and when I kissed him, he tasted of rain.

I SAID IT TO SEÁN ONCE – I said, if it had not been for Evie, we would not be together – and he looked at me as though I had just blasphemed.

'Don't be silly,' he said.

As far as he is concerned, there is no cause: he arrived in my life as though lifted and pushed by a swell of the sea.

In which case, Evie's room is like something after the tide went out: dirty feathers, scraps of paper, endless bits of cheap, non-specific plastic, and some that are quite expensive:

'Do you know how much those fucking things cost?' says Seán, going through the compacted filth of the Hoover bag, looking for a game from her Nintendo.

My stuff, on the other hand, does not matter. A Chanel compact, skittering across the floor, my phone pushed off the arm of the sofa, the battery forever after temperamental.

'Gawd,' says Evie.

She does not say 'sorry', that would be too personal.

Evie was always a bit of a barreller, a lurcher; her elbows are very close to her unconscious. At one stage they were going to have her checked for dyspraxia, by which they just meant 'clumsiness', but I guarantee you I have seen her move with great finesse. In this house, she is only clumsy around things that belong to me.

She eats nothing she is asked to eat, and everything that is forbidden. But she eats. Which I consider a minor miracle.

She filches, she sneaks and crams. She waits – a bit like myself, indeed – until her father is not there. The place we meet most often is at the fridge door.

Two months ago, when Seán was at the gym and Evie was complaining I had finished all the mayonnaise, I tossed my bag on the kitchen table and said, 'Why don't you go and buy your own fucking food?'

Not pretty, but true.

Evie looked at me, as though noticing me for the first time. Later that day, she said something to me – something that wasn't just a whine, like, 'Why don't you have Sky TV?'

She said, 'I can't believe you have so many shoes.'

And I had to leave the room to stuff my knuckles in my mouth, and pretend to bite into them, behind the door.

I LOOK FOR MY HIKING BOOTS and find them eventually on a shelf, wrapped up in a paper bag that came all the way from Sydney. I have not worn them since: my life, it seems, took the kind of turn that can only be effected in high heels. I take them out of the bag and the red dust of Australia shakes out on to our kitchen floor. My dreaming boots. I put them on and walk outside.

The afternoon snow has a shining crust that gives underfoot as I cross the garden and open the gate and join all the other tracks on the path into town. The slush has frozen back to ice in the shade and the difficulty pulls my eyes constantly downwards. I take one treacherous step after the next, and for the first while, I can not shake the rant.

It's hard, taking second place to a child – it was bad enough taking second place to her mother – and I remember what Seán said about me in his report to Rathlin Communications (now deceased – the ironies in that), when I took a sneaky look, and read where he had written – there was much praise there too, of course – that I was 'most ideally suited to a secondary role'.

That stung.

They underestimate me, I think. They underestimate my tenacity.

On Rathmines Road there is grit under my feet and the paths are walked clear. There aren't many cars, but the buses are running, and they leave moraines of dirty slush on either side of the road.

I pass the Observatory Lane, a shanty row of shops, Black-Berry Lane; the rugby pitches in front of St Mary's glutted with snow. The clouds have cleared, the sky is high and blue, the green dome of Rathmines church is still capped with white. The canal cuts a clean line under the bridge, the black water reflects the frozen water on its banks, and I am glad of the fresh air, my dreaming boots walking me into Dublin town. I remember the first Aborigine I saw, after maybe a week in Sydney, how very black he was and how very poor: you travel so far to realise that it's all true, all of it, like my father in his last days, *It is just as you always suspected.*

But we weren't wrong to hope, myself and Conor, back in our Australian days. And I am not wrong to hope, now: to hold on to Seán, and love him, and to try to love his daughter.

SHE IS THERE AT THE BUS STOP, as arranged, talking on the phone. I recognise her immediately and then see, afterwards, what she is: a schoolgirl who is not allowed to walk down a city-centre street alone – not even in the snow, when the monsters that wait for schoolgirls surely have other things on their minds. I feel like taking her drinking. I feel like telling her to get out now, while the going is good. Not bother growing up.

Turn back! It's a trap!

She spots me and puts away the phone. I see that she is wearing, on this cold day, almost nothing. A short denim skirt, opaque tights, a little black cotton jacket, a gingham scarf with added bobbles and metallic threads. Her only concessions to the freezing weather are black fingerless gloves and Ugg boots. Maybe her coat is in her backpack. I can only imagine the fight before she left the house.

'Uggs!' I say, coming up to her. 'It comes to us all.'

To which she gives a long-suffering smile.

I am beginning to understand Evie's silences, which come in many varieties. Her chat, on the other hand, is endlessly the same: hard to listen to and harder still to remember. I don't know how Seán stays sane. It is mostly comprised of opinions, as she sifts through likes and dislikes of the kind you can choose on MTV: I don't like this, I really like that. My friend Paddy says she really likes this, and I'm like, 'How can you like that?' This is mixed with scenes from movies, some small problems about the future of the planet, and some large problems about the dragon game she used to play online but doesn't now because no one is *into* that anymore. She is into being *into* things. She is majorly *into* unfairness – an ardent egalitarian, anti-designer label, anti-bullying – her friend Paddy, she says, agrees with her about all of this (her friend Paddy, she says, in pretty much the same breath, *always* travels business class).

I feel that the world might be better if it was run by girls who are nearly twelve, the ability they have to be fully moral and fully venal at the same time. Capitalism would certainly thrive.

'Do you want to look around the shops?' I say, and get a response that is alert, almost animal.

'OK.'

'Where do you want to go?'

A look around the shops means, it turns out, for Evie, a look at shops that sell cheap soap; either ecologically aware, or freshly made.

We walk across to Grafton Street in silence.

'You got the bus OK?'

Until we pass a baby in a little pram.

'Ngaaawww,' she says.

Evie's interest in babies is so keen, it might be cause for concern, except for the fact that she is twice as interested in dogs.

She can not pass a baby without living a moment in their skin: 'He doesn't like the cold,' she says, or, 'Her hat is over her eyes,' or just, 'Ngawww!' I think she is unusual in this, and I don't know where it will all end.

'Did you hear from your Dad?'

'Em.'

'Did he say when he was going to be home?'

'I think he said he was on the plane.'

I leave her to the rows of smelly bottles; the untwiddling of caps, the sniffings and little rubbings that the shop requires. Moisturisers, toners, exfoliators: she is out of her depth, I realise, and a little disappointed by it all.

'I think it's time,' I say. 'To up your game.' And I bring her down the street and into one of the posh shops, and a rack of perfume that she studies with quiet intent. The one she chooses finally is called Sycomore, which is so much the one my mother would have chosen, it makes me feel misplaced and odd.

'My mother liked that,' I say.

And she gives me a sidelong glance, as if to say that people my age should not have mothers. As, indeed, I do not.

'My mother,' I continue, because I am trying to push my way through something here, 'wouldn't buy it, of course. She would just try it – like every time she came into town – and then decide it wasn't, you know, right.'

'Cool,' says Evie.

A fabulously tall sales girl rounds on us, walking past.

'Yes? You would like to refresh yourself?'

Evie waves the bottle in vague apology, saying, 'I'm just having a free go.'

And we move on; me pushing the small of her back, both of us trying not to laugh.

I bring her to the MAC counters, and she looks at me like this could not possibly be allowed. But I don't care. She is tall enough now to pass for any age, if she wanted to – if, that is, she could just get the expression right, on her big, honest face.

It is Friday afternoon and, despite the weather, the place is stuffed. We are in a ruck of girls moving in slow motion towards and away from a maze of upright mirrors, turning their uncertainty into a stroke of this, a dab of that. They switch to the next brush and potion, then lean slowly in again: predatory, rapt.

'You know what you want?' I say.

Evie heads straight for a bank of foundation, picks one about two shades too pale, and she plies the brush, really working it in. I wonder what bedroom rituals led to all this expertise – I suspect Paddy's dread hand – as she refuses highlighter, blusher, bronzer, to go for powder that is paler yet, and thick eyeliner.

'Fabulous,' I say.

All this while I try two different foundations, same shade, different texture, one on either cheek.

She selects an eyeshadow of deepest purple because, she says, it will make her eye colour 'pop'.

I never know whether Evie will be good-looking. I squint a bit, trying to guess how she might morph over the years; the nose a bit stronger, the chin firmer. But I can't hold it: her changing features drift away from each other and her future face falls apart.

All children are beautiful: the thing they do with their eyes that seems so dazzling when they take you all in, or seem to take you all in; it's like being looked at by an alien, or a cat – who knows what they see? So Evie is beautiful because she is a child, but she is pretty ordinary looking too. The make-up brings it out in her – perhaps for the first time – her cheekbones will never be up to much, I think, and the nose is a bit of a blob. Though she still has those lovely, watchful eyes.

'Is Megan into make-up?' I say.

'What?'

'Megan. My niece.'

She doesn't answer. Perhaps the relationships are too hard for her to draw. Then she says, 'Actually Megan's really into manga at the minute.'

'Don't do that,' I say. She has unscrewed a lipstick that is so purple it is almost black.

'No?'

'No.'

'Why not?' *Because your father will kill me.*

'They might have cold sores.'

She looks me in the eye. 'No they won't!'

She is suddenly, immediately, spoiling for a fight. I have a glimpse of what her mother has to put up with these days – only I get the opposite. I get it flipped into:

You're not my mother!

Such violent emotion. And I have no reply.

She is quite correct: it was a stupid thing to say, and I am not her mother. I have no rights here. I can not mirror her mood, or throw it back at her. I see the next few years of my life, just taking whatever she wants to sling at me; a mute receptacle for her hate.

I say, 'Wow, blue mascara.'

Evie puts the lipstick down.

'Where?'

I slip off and buy the eyeliner for her – as a bribe, I suppose (more blood money), but it works. She is delighted. Evie was always easy to please and adolescence has not changed that. She scrubs off most of the make-up – 'It always looks better after you've slept in it,' I say – and we walk back to Dawson Street talking about tattoos, ear piercing, hair dye and the number of points you need to get into veterinary these days.

'Your Mum,' I say, in a palliative way, at least once. Possibly twice. Maybe three times.

'What does your Mum say?'

'I'd ask your Mum about that.'

'I don't think your Mum would like it.'

The zombie wife is back.

It is freezing cold. I bring her into a coffee shop for take-out and realise, in the queue, that she is too young for coffee.

'Sometimes I have peppermint tea.'

I think I used to drink coffee at her age, certainly tea – I might be wrong. My mother is dead so I have no one to put me right on this.

After much peering at labels and signs, Evie settles on a hot chocolate. She takes her purse out of her backpack, and roots in it for money.

'No, you're all right.'

I pay at the till, remembering the day Aileen emptied out their joint bank account – what fun that was. How did she rear such a clear-hearted girl?

It is strange to me that Evie does not remember herself as

a child, and I do remember her: Evie in Fiona's garden, Evie on the beach. It is like she is always giving herself away, and keeps so little back for herself.

I hand her the hot chocolate and take her bag, and because it looks so cold outside, we tuck ourselves in at a table, and talk about dogs.

Evie says that when her Dad was growing up, he had a red setter that would steal eggs and his mouth was so soft and gentle, he could bring one home without cracking the shell.

'Really,' I say.

There is something so formal about talking to children: you have to be very polite. It is the only thing they understand.

'Do you know how to train a guard dog?' she says.

'No, I don't actually. Do you?'

Evie is always correcting herself. This is because everything she says comes out in the wrong order.

'When my Dad was little and they had a dog. Somebody had a dog and they locked it in the boot of a car. And on the first day they passed the boot and the dog barked and on the second day they tapped on the boot and the dog went crazy and on maybe the fourth day—'

'Four days?' I say.

'I know,' she says. 'On the fourth day the dog was completely silent and they opened the boot.'

Then she starts again.

'No, the *new* owner of the dog. If you want the dog to change owners. Because a guard dog is trained to protect just one person and attack anyone else. So they give the new owner a piece of meat and he has to go up and open the boot.'

'Jesus.'

'And the dog can hardly see or anything because he's been in the dark, and he just takes the meat, and he licks your hand, and then the dog loves you for the rest of his life.'

'He told you this?'

'Yes.'

'Your father?' I said.

'What?'

'Did your father do this to a dog?'

'When he was growing up.'

'Who locked the dog in the boot?'

'I don't know who *did* it,' she says.

I look at this child and think about the days and weeks, the months of my life I have spent waiting for her father to call me. Is this something she should know?

I want to tell her that I sat outside her house in the dark one night, hanging on to the steering wheel, while she slept sixty feet away. I imagined her father behind those stone walls, I could not move for the intensity of my imagining: Seán in one place or another, doing something, or another thing, that was hard to sense or describe. I spent hours willing myself into him. And, you know, he might not even have been there.

'So, give me some more dogs,' I say.

'My Dad?'

'Yeah. Why not?'

'His Mum had a springer spaniel and he ran out under a car and she said she was too sad ever to get another one ever again.'

'Your Gran?'

'My Nana.'

'Right. Do you like your Nana?'

'What?'

Seán would kill me, if he heard me ask her this. It is a great violation and I really quite enjoy it. I don't know what I am stealing, but it is candy from a baby, I know that.

'I mean what is she like, your Nana?'

'My Nana?'

'Is she a bit mean?'

'What?'

And I want to lean across the little table and say, 'Your father is not the man you think he is.'

I don't of course, I say, 'How's the hot chocolate?'

'Mmmn.'

There is no need to tell Evie about her father. She knows him better than anyone, because she loves him better than anyone. The facts about him – his kisses and his lies, his charm and his misdeeds – what are they to Evie?

What are they to me?

I say, 'I remember you when you were just a little thing.'

'Yeah?'

'Long before your father and me. I mean long before anything. You were just.'

'What was I like?'

I look at her. Seán's pupils are ringed with a gold so pale it is nearly white. In Evie's, the grey gives way to a burst of amber, quite intense.

'You were very like yourself, actually.'

'What age was I?'

'Four or five.'

She looks out the window.

'There's videos,' she says. 'But we have the wrong charger.'

'You were super-cute.'

'Was I? I think the videos were for the doctor mostly.'

'Well, everyone was very worried about you, sweetie.'

I have an urge to kiss her, just where her black hair gives way, and the skin of her ear shades into the skin of her cheek.

I ask her does she remember being sick and she says that she does, though I don't know if this can be true – she was, after all, only four. She says, 'I had this horrible feeling in my stomach, like I had done something wrong, and then, Bam. I used to think a giant stomped on my head. But just before, just a second before, it was really nice. It was like, "Here it comes. Here comes the foot."'

'You must have got it from "fit". Here comes the "fit".'

She is silent.

'We don't say "fit",' she says. 'We say "seizure".'

'Yes of course,' I say (because you have to be so polite with children). 'I'm sorry.'

'But I didn't do anything wrong.'

'No of course you didn't.'

'I mean it made me so cross. I wet my pants and everything.'

'Finish up your drink, there. We'll go.'

She holds the paper cup in two mittened hands and drinks, leaving a shallow V of chocolate flaring from her upper lip. She watches me, over the edge of the cup. She says, 'What's "Gina" short for?'

'Nothing. My mother just liked it.'

'It's nice.'

'Thank you.'

Evie will be all right, I think. Despite everything. Despite all our best efforts, you might say, the child has come good.

WE GO OUT ON to the street and look up at a dark sky, sifting snow.

'Will we take a cab?' I say. 'For the hell of it.' But Evie says, 'My Dad isn't back at the house yet.'

'Where do you want to go?'

'Well, *I* don't know.'

'Let's walk for a while. You want to walk?'

I take her backpack and we head up to Stephen's Green. We go in a side gate and start to cross the park, aiming for the bus stop on Earlsfort Terrace. We don't talk much. Evie slides along on the soles of her boots in a way that would annoy me, if I were her mother, but it does not annoy me much.

I go through the darkening town with Seán's beautiful mistake. Because it really was a mistake for Seán to have a child, and it was a particular mistake for him to have this child; a girl who looks out on the world with his grey eyes, from a mind that is entirely her own. Lovers can be replaced, I think – a little bitterly – but not children. Whoever she turns out to be, he is forever stuck with loving Evie.

I think I love her myself, a little.

Her phone beeps and I know it is him, landed at last. It takes her an age to set her bag down and unpack it to find the phone, and read his text. (I wait for my phone to jump but it does not.)

'He'll be, like, forty minutes,' she says.

The snow will melt, the houses will sell – one house, or the other – and Evie will grow or be otherwise lost to me. Not that I ever had her, really. But whether her father stays with me or goes, I will lose this girl.

I say, 'I know it's hard about your parents, Evie.'

She does not reply.

'I just think, it was going to happen one way or another. I mean it could have been anyone, you know?'

She slides on; one scraping step after the other.

'But it wasn't,' she says.

I can't quite see her face.

'It was you.'

ACKNOWLEDGEMENTS

MANY THANKS TO GERALDINE DUNNE of Brainwave, the Irish Epilepsy Association, and to my old friend, Aideen Tarpey, now with the NHS, for chat and information about epilepsy in children: all errors of fact or emphasis are, of course, my own.

THANKS TO LIA MILLS for reading early chapters and cheering me on.

THANKS TO EVERYONE AT Rogers, Coleridge and White, to the people at Random House and, as ever, to my agent Gill Coleridge and to Robin Robertson, my editor these many years.

A NOTE ABOUT THE AUTHOR

ANNE ENRIGHT WAS BORN IN DUBLIN and graduated from Trinity College, Dublin, with a degree in English and philosophy and from the University of East Anglia with an MA in creative writing. Enright's short stories have appeared in *The Paris Review*, *Harper's*, and *The New Yorker*, and she writes frequently for *The Guardian*. Her first novel, *The Wig My Father Wore*, was published in 1995 and was shortlisted for the Irish Times/Aer Lingus Irish Literature Prize. Her fourth novel, *The Gathering*, received the Man Booker Prize for Fiction in 2007. Enright has also received the Rooney Prize for Irish Literature and has been a writer fellow at Trinity College. She lives in Bray, Ireland, with her husband and two children.